I0640086

MASTER ME

THE ATLAS COLLECTION (BOOK 2)

SAPPHARIA MAYER

EIDYLLIO

This is a work of fiction. Names, characters, businesses, places, events, locales, and incidents are either the products of the author's imagination or used in a fictitious manner. Any resemblance to actual persons, living or dead, or actual events is purely coincidental.

Ebook ISBN: 978-1-64893-003-4

Audiobook ISBN: 978-1-64893-005-8

Print ISBN: 978-1-64893-004-1

AUTHOR'S NOTE

Dear reader,

I am so glad you picked up my book, and I hope you enjoy the story it weaves. Please remember, theses books are works of fiction. The timelines are compressed, the interactions are dramatic and characters often jump into things for want of adventure.

You, dearest reader, live in a reality where the world is often stranger than fiction and a good dominant or submissive is hard to find. When you do find one, it is quickly evident they are imperfect humans who can't read minds, are less observant than one might prefer, and the interaction with them takes time. Like all things in life, communication is the key to any good interaction. The more authentically open you can be with a partner the more fulfilling the relationship.

Remember you are in charge of your life. Use your safe word, let others know where you are, know what aftercare looks like for you, use protection and have fun. The goal is to live in a beautiful safe, sane and consensual relationship with all parties pulling their weight. It is my hope you all find your special someone, just like the characters in my books. ***~Sappharia***

WARNINGS & DISCLAIMERS

Warning:

This book contains sexually explicit scenes and adult language. It may be considered offensive to some readers. This book is for sale to adults only, as defined by the laws of the country in which you made your purchase.

Disclaimer:

Please do not try any new sexual practice, without the guidance of an experienced practitioner. Neither the publisher nor the author will be responsible for any loss, harm, injury, or death resulting from use of the information contained in this book.

CHAPTER ONE

"God, they are hot when they play." Samantha leaned over and nodded her head to a couple playing on the St. Andrew's Cross on the other side of the pool. "I wonder if the hot one swinging the flogger will play with me afterwards?"

"Really?" Sarcasm dripped off her reply as Jillian followed Samantha's gaze. "That's your boyfriend and one of his other partners."

She grinned. "Yeah. Aren't they hot? I'm hoping I can seduce them both in bed."

Jillian shook her head. There was no such thing as too much information between them, but Samantha's extreme love life always made her feel naïve. She guessed it came from the ability to explore everything that piqued her interest.

"Why are people such animals?" Samantha moaned and stood. "Alexandra will be pissed if she comes back to a club that needs repairs. I need to find Kade and see if he can those guys under control. Wish me luck!"

She started toward the pool deck and glanced back with a forced smile. "And stop looking like you're miserable."

Jillian shook her head. For the past two hours, she'd perched on a bar stool watching everyone have a delightful time while she wondered why she hadn't stayed home. With a discouraged sigh, she scanned the club's bar and lounge. The refinement environment sat a juxtaposition with the small groups of people in various levels of undress gathered around the room. In front of the bar, large garage-style glass doors rolled up to make the space flow from inside to the outside. Everything about it was in total opposition to the standard concepts of a BDSM club, but then again, it was one reason Samantha had invited her as a guest. She'd used the excuse of painful elegance as enticement.

On a lounge chair, a muscular brunette caught her attention as his firm hands moved across the body of a woman. He straddled her as he massaged her shoulders. A leather cord with a sterling silver bead hung around his neck in a subtle nod to his position or ownership by Mistress or Master. On the bootblack stand, a man in a white tank top and Levi jeans sat while the boi in front of him made his boots shine in the setting sun. In the pool, couples and groups laughed and made out, unfazed by their au natural appearances.

While certain things would signal the obvious, it was often hard to tell who among the groups were dominants. She'd learned long ago that appearances and positions could be deceiving. Just because someone looked like they were the take charge in the bedroom type, it didn't mean it was true. All around her was evidence of someone, no matter how unlikely, falling to their knees for the right person.

Jillian took a long sip of wine. The trouble was finding the right person. To the world, Jillian was a take no prisoners with her shit together type of girl who could take care of herself. On the inside, she knew the right combination would make her melt, but the likelihood of finding him seemed slim in the sea of players.

She set the empty glass down and nodded to the bartender. Her stomach growled in protest against the corset which hugged her body into a tight hourglass figure. A few minutes later, he returned with a full glass of wine and a bowl of bar snacks. He set them down in front of her and smiled.

"I bet you haven't eaten all day," he said.

"How'd you guess?"

"With a corset that tight, you can barely breathe, let alone eat." He shoved the bowl of bar snacks closer to her. "At least eat this. I won't have you passing out on the barstool and leaving me to explain to Security how I fell down on my job. Especially if I let a gorgeously corseted lady land ungraciously on her rump. Besides, I don't want such a report hitting Alexandra's desk. She'd have my hide for it." His Texas drawl was unmistakable and it made her smile at his concern.

From the way Samantha talked, Alexandra was a force to be reckoned with. The club's owner and house dominant was usually at events, but her sudden disappearance had caused quite a stir. The staff did a fabulous job keeping it hushed, explaining she'd taken an extended vacation, but from Samantha's worried expressions and the private conversations carried on in hushed tones, no one had any clue where she'd gone.

On the other side of the room, she spotted Samantha bent toward a guy in a basic T-shirt and jeans, gesturing in her general direction. She'd never been able to convince Samantha she wasn't into the fun and fancy-free ways. It was fun to watch her friend take in the world with such a free spirit, but she could never let herself give up such control.

At the conclusion of their conversation, Jillian watched the man approach. From afar, his wild goatee appeared wicked and sexy. She reached for her wine, straightened her shoulders, and tried to appear calm, cool and confident, even as butterflies assaulted her stomach.

"You must be Jillian." Her name slid off his tongue in a low rumble.

"Um. Yeah," she stuttered.

Up close, he was far less appealing. He was young in the casual way of someone who came into money but didn't care about standard conventions.

"Samantha said I should introduce myself and I am so glad she did too." He leered, appraising her from top to bottom. She wasn't the front of the magazine beautiful, but she expected others to care more about their appearance than the man in front of her. If she put in the effort, so should they.

"And you are?" Her words came out with more distaste than she intended.

"Evan."

"Nice to meet you, Evan." Jillian shifted on her barstool as he moved to take the one next to her.

The potent scent of his cologne almost choked the air from her lungs. Why did guys always think they needed to pour it on to 'smell sexy'?

He looked over to the bartender who nodded and set a glass of bourbon on the bar in front of him.

"What brings you here this evening?"

"Samantha. She dragged me here demanding that I 'make play happen.'"

Jillian forced a smile.

"Well that sounds like a fun proposal. What do you say we find out what that means?"

Her face flushed. When he put it that way, she felt cheap and incapable of finding what she wanted without Samantha's intervention. Or was she being too picky? Wanting a specific type of person who wasn't up for a constant game of kinky catch and release.

Jillian shrugged and let her gaze fall across the room, unsure how to respond. The situation was far more awkward than she could imagine. Couldn't someone approach her like a human? Get to know each other, find out if they were compatible and not just go after the 'fuck me now' parts?

"What things would you like me to get into?" Evan continued, unfazed by her lack of response.

Other than wanting a person who wanted to know her, understood what made her tick, and even realized what would make her melt into a moment of pure bliss, she did not understand what she wanted in the scene anymore. Her private browser was full of darker ideas of domination, and she'd explored areas she never thought would turn her on but made her body race at the mere thought.

Ever since joining social sites for kinksters, she couldn't count the number of cock shots or men begging for her to be their Mistress. Maybe she should take them as compliments because they believed she was hot and a strong independent woman who could handle her own life.

Right next to her sat all of those things in the flesh, and every one of those unsolicited emails was suddenly right in her face. All he was offering her was uncommitted physical play--the thing Samantha told her to embrace with both hands and loosen up.

"I'm not sure what I want," Jillian said, hedging on an honest answer. "I've been out of the scene so long I feel rather like a voyeur and a virgin."

Samantha and her partners were the reason she'd ventured into the club at all. She loved to sit on the sidelines as they played. The dynamics were both overt and subtle. You had to be observant to catch everything that went on between them. Her newest partner, Trey, had a trained eye to keep her to heel. He knew which buttons he could push. The slightest arch or furrow of his eyebrow would cause her cheeky mouth to slam shut or make her walk to him like a magnet when he crooked his finger. Her partner Saul was a sensualist who put her body in a state of pure bliss. His style of domination was soft and subtle, just under the surface. Then there was her girlfriend, Chelsea, who fed her need for the softer, funny, feminine, sexy side. Finally, there was her husband, who had his own set of lovers, and loved to see Samantha happy.

Jillian would never wrap her head around how Samantha juggled so many relationships. Her chosen family seemed functional and contented with the arrangement. On the other side, she couldn't even find one person who filled her baser needs.

Every time she tried to let herself go, her strong, independent, feminist self would yell at her for the traitorous way she wanted to submit to a man. She wanted to let go, to let someone else take control for a while. The word causing her much angst was trying rather than doing. Jillian struggled to be unapologetically in touch with her own sexuality, but doubts always crept in on the idea that another person would earn her submission. Even if those wicked fantasies of force and control starred in most of her sessions with BOB, her battery-operated boyfriend, she'd been in the scene long enough to know that the fantasy and reality were often far apart.

Evan shifted on the barstool next to her, drawing Jillian's attention to him. "Everyone has fantasies they want to live out. We need to find out where to start and go from there. Do you like pain, dominance, being fucked in front of a crowd, sucking lots of men off at once?"

Jillian grimaced at the disconnected images which rose in her head as his words played across her brain. Not the shy and coy type, Evan's directness made her blush, and she grabbed for her wineglass.

"That's a very sex-based place to start," she commented without looking at him.

"Well, Samantha said you were looking for a fun, sexy time. I thought we might skip all the 'Get on your knees' bits and go right to the fun 'do me' parts." He waggled his eyebrows.

She sat there stunned. How had a conversation gone from 'Hi' to 'You wanna fuck?' in record time? Where was the small talk, the personal conversation? She wanted to trust someone to take her anywhere and anytime, inflicting a little pain. Her top ten fantasies whirled through her head, but she wasn't ready for pickup play at the same level.

The photos she browsed of women bound outside, blindfolded and waiting at the feet of a man with her head in his lap, made Jillian hot. The concept of giving control was amazing in theory, but there was no way she could ever make it a reality. It didn't help that she would call someone on their shit and stand toe to toe. No matter how much she wanted the tendrils of dominance to wrap around her once again, the armor she wore did not bode well for any level of deep submission.

Samantha often pushed Trey, but he enjoyed her slightly bratty nature, allowing the cheekiness to go so far before yanking her back to a more submissive place. It was a fascinating process from the sidelines. It often made Jillian wonder what it would be like for someone take her in hand and make her crave the submission. She longed to experience the emotions coursing through Samantha when she had a blissed-out state on her face again. To connect to another person in a way which made the synchronicity appear to happen by magic. A place where, no matter what they asked, her best interests and desires were at the heart of it.

"I don't know. I'm not really the casual fucking type," she answered to fill in the interminable pause.

"Really?" Evan's body stiffened, his shoulders straightening as he leaned in toward her. A glint in his eyes told her he was the type to rise to a challenge, not be put off by it. "I love making a mouthy girl mumble with my cock in her face hole."

Jillian worked to stop the automatic eye roll. Several men she'd encountered on dating and kinky sites seemed to want to break a girl and then leave the pieces behind. They wanted the conquest and not the prize. She didn't want to be with anyone who wasn't invested in her as much as she was invested in him. Was it too much to ask that a man be a gentleman who loved to take control and put her in her place, on occasionally? Too many romance novels let her conjure up the perfect hot bad boy image in her mind, and she sighed. Maybe Samantha was right. She wanted a relationship. Yet she had no relationship. Perhaps she needed to lower her too-high expectations to find one.

"Watch the teeth in that scenario," she warned.

"Mmm. You are feisty. Let's go down to the private rooms and see what it takes to get you on your knees begging for my cock."

"I don't think so." She frowned.

"Why not? The club does free STD testing, they vet everyone

and my status is easy to pull up. You know I'm 'safe.'" His fingers air quoted on safe, throwing an immediate red flag for Jillian.

"It's too soon to just walk downstairs and give you a blowjob, no matter how 'safe' you are," she replied, mimicking his previous movements.

"I thought you were here to have a magnificent time. I can make your body feel so good you will forget your own name when I'm done."

Jillian worked to school the shocked look.

"This could be your only chance to sample all this hot maleness. Live your deepest fantasies with no strings attached. Haven't you wanted to do that for a long time?"

The whole situation was going way too fast and in all the wrong directions. Who just walks up to someone and expects to have sex with them?

"Come on, hot stuff, the private rooms are just down the stairs. I can reserve one and open your eyes to a whole new set of fantasies."

She shook her head. "I'm sure you're a great guy..."

Evan snapped in frustration before she could complete the rejection. "My patience only goes so far, bitch."

Warning bells sounded in her mind and she was glad her wineglass was in her hand throughout the entire conversation. This guy knew nothing about her except the conquest he wanted between her legs.

"Bitch? Really? So not interested." She slid off her barstool, and he followed suit. He was easily three inches shorter when his feet hit the floor.

He looked up and growled. "Yeah. Bitch. I thought this is what you wanted, you cock tease. What's your problem? Not good enough in bed?"

"Isn't it obvious? Her problem is you," a male voice said from behind her and she noticed the body heat radiating off his nearness.

She turned around and let her eyes follow the wall of muscles and tattooed arms up to the face of the man. The angry expression on his face was menacing as he looked down at Evan. Jillian stood, unable to move, between the two men.

"Why don't you fuck off? The lady and I were getting down to some sexy business."

From behind her, the man stepped around Jillian and toward Evan. His body relaxed, but the air rippled with tension as the two men faced off.

After several long minutes, Evan shrugged. "You can have her. She's just a cock teasing mouthy bitch, anyway."

CHAPTER TWO

He turned and walked toward a group already in a whispered hush who'd watched the entire scene. Jillian let out a deep sigh of relief until the man glanced back, and his dark blue eyes locked on her. The world stood still between the seconds. At this moment, she wondered what it would be like to beg him for all the things in her head, and a few she hadn't yet explored.

As suddenly as it surrounded her, his commanding presence shrank away and a soft smile tipped up the corners of his mouth.

"May I join you?" He gestured to the seat Evan had been perched on moments before.

"Sure," she croaked, cleared her voice, and forced the word out again.

"Kade, the imposing guy leaning on the doorframe." His head flicked to a sizable man in dark pants and a tight black T-shirt with Security in bright yellow letters embossed across his chest. "He's the head of Security and asked me to come over here to ensure everything was okay. No doubt you had the situation under control, but the conversation was making the bartender uncomfortable. No one should pressure someone else into things they don't want."

She nodded.

Something about him that held her rapt attention.

"No should mean no, whether one is discussing sex or play. You shouldn't feel pressured to give in to anything you don't desire."

"This is all so much more complicated than I remember, or maybe it's just me. I regret even thinking about stepping into this world again."

"Why do you regret thinking about it?" He quirked his eyebrow.

"I used to believe this fantasy could be made real. That walking back into a different version of this world would yield diverse results."

Across the room, Samantha caught her eye and her expression contorted in shock, which morphed into a mischievous grin. The man beside Jillian studied her, unaffected by the silence between them. He smelled clean with a hint of musk. Everything about him was sexy as hell. The tight black shirt and jeans hugged his body in all the right places.

"Um, so why did Security send you over here? Are you on staff?"

He chuckled. "The head of Security and I have been friends for years. He's got his hands full of some unusual issues and I know how to handle Evan."

A long silence filled the space and undesired thoughts spun in Jillian's head. Too many times she'd gotten her hopes up that this would be the One, and they'd walked out the door when she'd been 'too much' for them. On several occasions someone had called her a brat or accused her of topping from the bottom and trying to run things when she'd given her input. Yet here she sat, letting her mind dream of the possibilities again.

Needs clawed their way to the surface. Finding her perfect match was complicated, which is why this adventure was supposed to be an attempt to venture out to play and have fun, but that wasn't her make-up. Without a doubt, Jillian understood why she was such a relationship failure.

There were so many other things she could be doing right now, like sitting on the couch watching mindless television, curled up with an enjoyable book or even the endless task list that comes with home ownership. The comfortable feeling of yoga pants and ice cream, rather than these stilettos and a stiff corset. Still, here she sat letting her mind run amok about a man who'd saved her from a total jerk.

"I need to pay rent on my tea," he said, breaking the tension as he jerked his head toward the restrooms.

He rose from the bar stool and her neck craned up as her gaze followed. Rarely did she meet a man much taller than herself. At right under six feet, most men looked up to her and in heels she often topped out several inches over. In her younger days, she crushed on every guy who met her eye to eye and chased everyone who met her internal height requirement, which was rare. His lame excuse to step away played over and over in her head as it fed every insecurity she'd stuffed down over the years.

Jillian forced a confident smile.

"Of course."

"I'll be right back," he said as he turned from the bar.

As he walked away, images danced across her mind at all the sad versions of the same situation she'd experienced over the years.

Her eyes settled on his tight ass and admired his entire body from the back. Too many times things had not gone well, and it was time to face the fact she'd be alone for a long time, but it didn't stop her from internally drooling at the eye candy walking away from her.

"That one's dangerous." Samantha's voice startled Jillian out of her reverie as she slid into the vacant seat.

"They are all dangerous. They are men. They want a conquest, then they walk away." She tried to sound lighthearted.

"What happened to Evan?"

"You mean, 'Hey you're cute, let's go downstairs and fuck?'"

She cringed the answer.

"He didn't."

"He did. You know I'm not a one-night stand, casual sex type of girl."

"Yeah, but I thought he'd suggest something a little less direct and creepy."

"Your help isn't helping, Samantha," Jillian said and tried to fake a laugh. "The head of Security, some guy named Kade, told Mister Tall, Enigmatic and Hot to 'save' me. Who the hell do they think I am, a damn princess?"

"Wait, Kade sent him over here to fix the situation?"

Jillian nodded.

"The bartender was becoming uncomfortable with the lack of 'no means no' thing."

"Oh shit."

Her eyes followed Samantha's gaze. The man who'd been leaning on the door frame was already in motion and walking toward them.

"What?" she asked, concern lacing her voice.

Before she could answer the question, Kade walked up and stood beside Samantha.

"Well, well, what do we have here?"

Samantha hesitantly smiled up at him, but Kade placed his hand on the back of the bar stool caging her between the bar and her seat.

"Are you the one who got Evan all fired up, promising him things you knew couldn't be delivered?"

"I didn't realize he'd take it like that, Kade," she cooed as she batted her eyelashes at him.

"We've been friends since college. That mischievous twinkle in your eye is obvious. What have you done this time, Samantha?"

"Nothing. I was trying to get this poor girl laid!"

"With Evan? You can't be serious."

There was an easy banter between them and a subtle tension that they both ignored, and Jillian felt like a voyeur in a private moment.

"I thought a couple magnificent orgasms would do her good. Give her a fresh perspective. Relieve stress," Samantha said as she pouted up at Kade.

He shook his head as he turned to watch the man walk back toward them.

"I'm sure Jillian can figure out how to get laid without your help. Besides, I've got news about Atlas. Let's go back to my office and talk."

"Is it..." she started.

"Office. Now. We will discuss the situation there," he snapped, and her mouth clamped shut. Worry filled her eyes. Interrupting them would not go well.

"We weren't formally introduced by the rude, yet kindhearted, Samantha. I'm Kade." He offered a quick handshake. "I hope we'll see more of you around here."

Jillian smiled and nodded as he placed his hand on Samantha's back and led her out of the lounge area. For a long time, she sat and stared after them, wondering at the whole interaction. So much worry clouded her friend's face.

Her thoughts were interrupted by the body heat of another person moving onto the barstool next to her. She shifted and turned out toward the lounge.

"So you're here to play?" he asked as he settled and watched her move away from him.

Her unrequested knight in shining armor had returned.

"I thought so, but I realized I don't know what I want anymore. I thought I could do the casual thing."

She glanced up at him. The snug black T-shirt enhanced the ink running up his arms. She felt small in his presence, which was a feat. She never felt small. Unable to curl up into a man's arms and hide from the world.

Jillian shook her head to cast away the unbidden thoughts and looked back at him.

"What brings you here? With a little duct tape and rope, you'd be dressed for the perfect kidnapping of a damsel in distress."

"Well, you are a damsel and I rescued you from distress." He smirked, arching an eyebrow.

"Oh, yes please." She tried to joke.

"Careful what you wish for, damsel." He grinned. "Here I thought you weren't up to playing tonight after your bout with Evan."

"Sometimes it is good to wish. It's like playing with universal level danger and hoping you survive."

Embarrassed by the easy banter, Jillian straightened up, causing the corset to catch her breath.

His gaze wandered over her bare shoulders, down her breasts to her waist, and traveled back up again. She could almost feel his touch following the same path over her body and shivered at the thought. The interaction made her feel self-conscious, and she pulled on the top of her corset.

"Very nice." His voice rumbled through his chest.

"I'm not usually the dress-up doll type."

"No? How unfortunate, it suits you." His eyes crinkled on the corners when he smiled.

Jillian let out a disgusted sigh. Even the genuine ones were pushy.

"I'm just teasing you. Relax. We're just talking. Besides, you're not my type."

"I see," she said.

"Don't get me wrong, you're gorgeous, but we aren't looking for the same things here."

It was the same sentiment every man seemed to express as they walked out the door. At least this time he was upfront about it, and he didn't even know her. This arrogant egotistical ass was making assumptions in a five-minute conversation after he thought he needed to save her from a bigger jerk.

"And what, pray tell, are you seeking?"

"A slave."

"You mean one of those mindless, not allowed to talk, sit on the furniture or interact with other people without permission types? You've got to be kidding."

He chuckled. "See? Not looking for the same things."

"That's pretty radical and hardcore. What about equality in the relationship?" She shrugged, frustrated at the turn of events. The knowledge of his desires moved him out of all potential places in her world. While visions of him towering over her helpless form, riding crop in hand, raced through her mind.

"It's not for everyone, there's no question about it."

"There's an understatement."

A sly smile spread across his face. "If you want help to weed out the assholes, I'll be glad to help. It can be a monumental challenge when you're looking for a new partner."

"I can handle myself."

"There's no doubt there, but I could always help vet them or scare them away if they get unruly."

Jillian laughed. "Do you offer every girl in the place your generous white knight services?"

"No. Only specific ones."

"Wait. You're serious?" She had thought he was joking and tried to give him an easy out.

"Yes, Jillian, I am."

"How did you know my..."

He smiled and turned his head. A clear cord ran up his neck to the earpiece in his ear.

"That's cheating."

He shrugged.

"I call it using the resources available."

"What's in it for you then? It seems like an enormous amount of work for no return."

"You're Samantha's friend, and she's been friends with Kade since college. Kade and I have been friends for a long time and what's important to him is important to me. By association, you are important. Besides, it's a good deed."

"So I'm just karmic insurance."

"One can't be too careful nowadays. There's an insurance for everything, you know."

"Okay, then I accept your policy as the karmic underwriter." She laughed.

"Let me give you my number and you can engage when you need me."

"Are you saying like an enforcer? My own on-call white knight?"

"The only thing white about me is my skin, love."

"So what are those digits?" Jillian said as she pulled out her phone. "Wait. I agreed to something and I don't even know your name."

"And that says so much." He grinned. "I am Ian."

"What last name should I type in my phone?"

"Breckenridge."

The name sounded familiar, but with so many well-to-do families in the greater DC metropolitan area, it wouldn't be surprising to find any of them here. "So what do you do, Ian Breckenridge?"

"This and that, classified under a businessman. And you?"

She moaned inwardly. Work should be a safe topic, but it always led to more questions. "I'm a counselor."

"Really? High school or college?"

"Neither. Sex."

"Come again?"

"They usually do," she replied at the unintended innuendo.

For a long moment they stared at each other, neither willing to break contact. Finally, Jillian looked away. He was the perfect combination. Hot, had his shit together, strong and kinky. It was too bad he was into the hardcore stuff of wanting a slave. It might be an amazing fantasy to get her off, but in reality she knew she'd never come close. Still, if he could help her wade through the creeps as she kissed frogs, it could be worth having a protector of sorts.

"I'll think it over," Jillian said. "The having a 'protector' part."

She blushed realizing the follow-up wording to her early one.

"I look forward to your call."

And I can't wait to wear BOB, my exceptional battery-operated boyfriend, out when I get home, she thought.

CHAPTER THREE

"How are things going for you?" Jillian asked as she shut the door to her office. "Are the urges subsiding?"

She turned toward Carl, who sat on the couch. The position of the desk in the corner of her office, off to one side, allowed for a more open feel when she met with her clients. Creating an environment which provided a more approachable interaction.

"No," he admitted but offered no further explanation.

"No? Most of the time the protocols work. Have you been doing all the exercises?"

Jillian worked with him for several years. While on the surface he appeared to have his life well together, underneath it ran a man who desired to control at such a level it was almost psychopathic. It was always a tenuous treatment, but the center needed his money and it kept his name out of the media. No one knew one of the most successful and powerful men in DC was a controlling sex addict. She cared about him. Still, he always made her nervous. To succeed in this case meant keeping his tendencies well in line.

"I want her." His voice wavered. "To be under her boot. To have her all to myself."

She looked up at him and tried to feel compassion. He'd never be able to feel genuine love. The abuse he'd suffered as a child made it impossible for him to separate reality from fantasy. He could have basic relationships and he was a genius in business. The man before her was a far cry from the one so many years ago. Then, he had been angry, volatile, abusive, and sexually destructive in every relationship. As they worked through his past pain, she tried to help him discover who he was underneath it. Along the way, she hoped he could form lasting relationships, even intimate ones.

"We've talked about that, Carl..." she said.

"Please call me "Edmund, Jillian. You know I changed it long ago to leave the past behind and remake myself. It is frustrating when you refer to a moniker which endured so much abuse as to put me in a place where even angels fear treading."

This set Carl, now Edmund, apart from her other patients. His mind was almost scarily brilliant and his patience notorious. When he had come to her group for counseling, they all signed non-disclosure agreements, which bound them even tighter than the strict HIPAA laws for patient privacy.

To the outside world, the man before her was every bit Edmund. He had no abusive past. His record was sealed since all of his known offenses and victimizations happened before his eighteenth birthday. Now, six years later, there seemed to be cracks in the successes she thought they'd made over the years.

Together they had worked through his many childhood traumas, with successes and failures along the way. To the outside world he had it all. Money and power cloaked his life in a mystery only a few were privileged to understand.

"Is this the same woman who we've discussed in the past?"

Edmund nodded. "She's stunning. I love the way she controls me, making me serve her with the smallest flick of her delicate wrist."

"You know you can't keep a woman like a bird in a cage."

"It's not a cage. I just don't want to share her with anyone else. She's so amazing and delicate, yet her command of me is fierce. To share her with the world dilutes the essence of the unique bond between us."

She watched his eyes drift to his hands, folded in his lap. He was in his own fantasy world where things worked just as he commanded them to do.

Jillian took a deep breath. "You can get these urges under control. We've worked out the ways to help you handle moments like this for the last several months. Just follow the steps and call when you need help."

"I asked her to marry me, you know."

Concern laced through Jillian. His fantasies were usually controllable, but such an escalation meant the current medication was not working well. It was a fine balance to walk between over-medicating, which would cripple his business mind and under-medication, which would allow the free-flowing tendencies to run out of control.

"What is her name?"

He looked up, his eyes growing dark. "She's mine. You can't have her."

"Edmund," Jillian's tone warned. "You need to share her name. No harm comes by speaking her name. I know you can be fearless in the face of everything. Trust me. Just speak her name."

Things always got dicey with a client when someone became an obsession. The fine line of protection versus privacy was sometimes crossed to save a life or keep another person from harm. Knowing the name also allowed the session to take a turn and hopefully remove them as the client's obsession.

"You seem to have your act together. You'd like her. She's strong, dominant, independent, and graceful. Everything I've ever wanted in a woman, just like you."

A shiver ran up her spine. Other people in her life had referred to her as an aloof, cynical workaholic who was far too driven to turn out better than her parents. From her own professional self-analysis she knew she had a fear of intimacy and trust. It was what made her able to sympathize with many of her patients.

The image of Ian's powerful arms wrapping her in a safe embrace crowded through her mind. He was someone she should be afraid to engage with, no matter how she doled out advice to be fearless and go down new roads. Jillian knew she would not take her own advice and let someone else help her find happiness. Reaching out to him felt like jumping off a cliff. Unlike her clients, she understood there was an enormous difference between the fantasies that ran through her head and the realities of the same situations.

She shook her head to collect her thoughts and refocus on the task at hand. With an unsteady hand, she smoothed down her skirt and looked at Edmund. "We all fear being alone. We all fear failure."

"I don't fail." His voice was eerily calm.

"Never failing raises the stakes in the game."

"Yes, and I play high stakes every day. Winning is how I made it to the top." He faked a smile and tried to relax against the couch.

"You can't hold another person captive for your desires, Edmund."

"I don't want to hold her captive. I want to give her everything. Every desire, every wish will be hers."

"And if she desired to leave?"

"She wouldn't. Why would she, when she is surrounded by the most luxurious things?"

"A gilded cage is still a prison."

For a long time Edmund sat in silence, gazing out the window. When times were good, and the obsessions weren't taking over his world, he was a pleasure. Their conversation ran down an extensive list of topics, and she enjoyed conversing with him.

She tried to catch his gaze and work to make him re-engage. "What recent books have you read?"

He rumbled a laugh and the tension in the air lessened. "I like your attempt at engagement."

Scowling, Jillian shifted in her seat. "It is why we are here, Edmund."

"You talk about fear and releasing the fear, but you don't take your words to heart. Why not?"

His question took her by surprise. A sly smiled wormed its way across his lips. "You talk about intimacy but there is no ring on your finger to signify commitment, no personal pictures on your desk, no signifier of any life outside these four walls."

"My personal life is not up for discussion."

"Yet my personal life is often what we discuss."

Averting his gaze, Jillian fought to gain control of the situation. His words sliced through her, cutting far closer to the truth than she'd ever admit. The amount of intimacy she experienced added up to reading kinky novels and playing with her vibrator. Every day she talked to clients about creating intimate relationships when in reality she was a fraud of the highest order. All talk, no walk. Normally she faced her fears and walked right through them, but with several failed relationships to her credit, she found herself more cautious.

"I see I've struck a nerve close to home," Edmund said.

Jillian stood and walked over to her desk, picking up her calendar. "Next week, same time?"

Edmund nodded. "Can you imagine how wonderful it would be to feel desired as much as I desire her?" he said as he rose from his seat.

She watched him walk out the door.

CHAPTER FOUR

Another email dinged across his screen. Ian ignored it and kept his eyes down on the unseen papers in front of him. His mind raced with the events at the club several nights before. Everything annoyed him and he stood to pace his office.

He was bored and restless in his personal life. Most of the time he could plunge into work and bury himself so deep it created a mass of reasons to never surface from it until he'd settled again. Three months ago he'd broken it off with Lisa, and while she was a sweet girl, he easily overwhelmed her. He consistently had to compromise his own needs to make it work. The ending was a mess, and he'd sworn off relationships once again.

Rolling up the sleeves of his shirt, he lay the monkey fist cufflinks on his desk. They reminded him of a woman helplessly bound in front of him in the simplicity of rope, and an evil smile crept across his face. Underneath the edge of his sleeve peeked the flaming tattoo which wrapped around to cover both shoulders and down his back to the waist. It was a story of every major event and relationship in his life. A tapestry of pain and pleasure.

He never let his business associates glimpse them. In a business suit he even looked like an uptight business executive. It comforted him to know they were underneath. A reminder of the two lives he lived on a daily basis. On one hand, the wholesome business executive who ran his family's vast holdings and chafed at his rebellions streak. It was his more authentic self that needed to find an outlet.

Fresh out of an accelerated education program, he'd taken up extreme sports to release his pent-up needs and explored the world of dominance and submission in his personal life. On the slopes he'd met Kade, who was then a submissive to Alexandra, a woman who was a force of nature. When she approached him with an investment opportunity in the Empyrean Club, a BDSM club for the wealthy and well to do, he'd taken the leap. While it was rare for it to make the financial gains he normally preferred, it fulfilled the return on investment at a more personal level.

After his parents died in an airplane crash, he'd been handed the reins of the company at the tender age of twenty-four. The flames of the wreckage still haunted his dreams. He'd been on the slopes in a rebellion against his father's wishes to take his place in the family business. Cell signal was spotty, and it was hours later when they reached him. The images on the news reports were gruesome. A flock of geese had flown into the path of the small jet and taken both engines out. He imagined his parents last moments. In that moment, his external rebellion ended and the accident drove him harder to make them proud even in death.

Ian's father had been a powerful businessman. He had taken their waning fortune and settled the family back on their feet. Now under Ian's guidance, the company was an industry leader in several fields and consistently growing. His two siblings depended on him to keep them moving forward. He'd traded his carefree life for one of control and focus. In return, they were able explore theirs in whatever direction they chose.

He stared out the window, deep in introspective focus. The door to his office opened and shut without his notice.

"Don't jump, it's not worth it." A voice across the room startled him.

Turning, he smiled at his best friend. "Well, well. Look what the cat dragged in. What brings you to the highest peaks of DC from the lowest dungeon depths?"

Kade forced a smile across his lips. "I wish it were a social call."

Ian's brows furrowed at the look on Kade's face, and he motioned him to the chairs in front of his desk.

"You look awful, man. What's going on?"

Kade ran a hand across his face and sighed. "I've been trying to keep this under wraps. We've been trying to make it appear as no major issue."

"Just say it already. All the suspense is unnecessary."

"Alexandra's missing."

The words hung in the room.

"Missing how? I thought she was on a long vacation."

"That's just the story we've been repeating to keep the club members settled. She's such a fixture and runs the place with a velveted iron fist, we've just been trying to hold it together."

"Back up. What happened?"

"That part is still unclear, but we don't suspect foul play though we can't rule it out either." Kade paused and stared out the window. Mixed emotions played across his face in never-ending waves. "A client of hers sent several threatening 'love letters' and flowers over the past couple of months after proposing marriage to her, which she declined."

"Let me guess. She didn't tell you she was being stalked."

A tight grimace crossed Kade's face, and he nodded. "I knew something was wrong, but I missed it. This whole mess is my fault, and now she's missing or...."

"Don't even go there. We'll find her."

Ian's guts twisted. He knew Kade and Alexandra had a relationship in their distant past, and while the dynamic no longer existed between them, Kade still cared deeply for her.

He stood up and walked around to his desk, turning to the computer and pulling up information sheets.

"You must know all the background facts. Alexandra isn't who she appears to be."

"I know," he replied.

"What do you mean you 'know'? What do you 'know' exactly?" Kade asked, his voice almost a low growl.

"Relax. Alexandra, or in my financial, Atlas Devereux is the same person. How that woman carries off so many well-crafted personas is beyond me."

Kade's body relaxed, and he moved to the chair across from Ian.

"Now, start from the beginning," Ian prompted.

"I won't bore you with details. My team will send over the reports. After a session with Edmund, he proposed marriage to her, which she declined. He became temporarily more aggressive, but we thought it was the end of it. A passing obsession. Then he sent her flowers and threatening notes. I had noticed several security breaches on the ground and brought them to her attention, but she brushed me off."

"You don't think she was taking the threats seriously?"

"I think the opposite. The more I pushed her about it, the higher her walls became, until she refused to engage on the subject. The last time I saw her, the Congress woman's case had just blow up all over the papers."

Ian nodded.

"I was the Congresswoman's campaign manager at the time. There's no way I missed that one. Samantha and I had a massive falling out over it."

"Well, when it happened, Reece Gabriel walked into her office and lost it. He called her a whore and That was the last time we saw her. It is like she walked off the face of the Earth. Her phones, her calendar, and her daily papers were all piled purposefully on her desk."

"Do you think she ran out of fear?"

"That was our first thought too, but everyone thought if that was true she'd be in touch. If I go to the police, it will blow all of her identities simultaneously and create a whole different storm. This town loves a scandal, even with all of its masks and secrets."

"You're getting cynical, my friend. Let's go to lunch and discuss this further. You look like you can use a break."

Kade smiled and got to his feet. "I haven't had an appetite much lately."

"Don't make me Dom your ass. You're not my type but for a friend..."

Kade chuckled. "I don't submit to men."

"Neither do I. That gives us something in common." Ian grabbed the phone off the desk, and it went off in his hand. "Where am I taking you to lunch?" He unlocked his phone, glancing down at the unfamiliar number.

"I should..." Kade started.

"Stop. Now. Lunch wasn't a suggestion. The choice of location was, but I guess I'll take care of it," he replied and looked down at the message.

Hey, it's Jillian. We met at the club the other night.

Immediately he texted back, a smile crossing his face.

I remember.

"I know that look. Let me guess, Jillian," Kade shot back.

"Um... yeah."

"Looks like I missed a magnificent show then."

"Nah. I offered to be her protector. That was days ago. I figured she blew me off."

I was wondering if you'd like to grab a coffee or a drink sometime.

"There's one I could see you training from scratch. Creating an interesting dynamic. From the way Samantha describes her, she can be intense."

Ian shook his head.

"As much as I'd like to go hunting, the only offer on the table was a protector."

The intensity in her eyes the first time she'd looked up at him filled his mind. He thought about her long hair and how it would feel wrapped around his hands as he pulled her back and exposed her. Everything about her called to his needs. She didn't need a protector any more than he did, but he wanted to do it, anyway. Wanted to take her to the depths of her darkest fantasies, bring her back to reality, and sink her into them again. He'd thought about her under his tutelage, learning each movement to perfection, his hand pushing and prodding her body until it molded for him, breaking nothing that made her.

Kade's eyes narrowed at him.

"Looks like the predator might have found a prey."

He stood up and walked to the door. Ian followed behind, head down to his phone.

Sounds great. Date/Time?

He hit SEND as his hip slammed into his desk. Swearing under his breath, he looked up to catch up with Kade.

"You obviously can't walk and text. Either that or you're a closet masochist and the desk is your top."

Ian glared at him as they walked through the door. His administrative assistant stared at them as they passed.

"Stop shocking the vanillas, Kade, it's not good form," Ian growled.

Kade's eyes crinkled and he let out a chuckle. They walked through the hallway. The phone in Ian's pocket buzzed again as the elevator doors opened. He glanced down and tripped over the crack between the elevator and floor, stumbling inside.

How about Pump and Grind Coffee and Bar off of K. Say, Tuesday at 4:30p?

He stood staring at the text. Of all the places she could have chosen, it was a place called Pump and Grind? Kade pushed the button, shaking his head at his friend. Ian stared at the phone, trying to come up with a clever response. His mind thought of all the positions he'd like to both pump and grind her. He could see her begging to come, wanting to crawl to him, her ass bright red with his handprint.

Careful. I could think of many things I'd like to Pump and Grind.

He could imagine the blush blossoming across her cheeks as she realized the innuendo. It was a nice little coffeehouse that turned into a bar in the evening. The eccentric crowd that gathered was always good for people watching and the music often featured the local up-and-coming artists.

OMG. LOL. It's just a place I hang out occasionally. I didn't mean to imply... I didn't want to worry about our conversation.

Kade led him off the elevator by his elbow and through the office building front doors. With every ounce of self-discipline, he reined in his thoughts and tried to let her off the hook without further embarrassment.

We should stop, before we both get in trouble with this conversation. Tuesday at 4:30p sounds great.

There was an interminable pause and Ian was sure she would write nothing back.

Thank you for saving me... again.

They walked a scant distance to the deli on the corner. His thoughts were in all the wrong places and trying to find all the reasons she wasn't right for him.

"You've got it bad," Kade chided, shoving Ian into a chair.

"She'd be better off with someone else. Someone less intense and strict. She seems like one of those nice, naïve wholesome types. Strong and independent but not into handing over real power."

"Don't you worry your pretty little head, Ian. That girl can take care of herself."

"Then why did you send me over to do the whole dark knight thing?"

"Because it's what Alexandra would have done. There's something about her that just fit."

"And now you're a matchmaker?"

Kade flipped him the bird in a good-natured joke.

"Just don't break her heart. Samantha would kill you and there will be nothing I can do to help you in that case."

"Fuck you, Kade."

"I am good, but you're not my type."

Both men laughed. The tension from earlier dissipated enough to settle the surrounding mood.

The waitress came by and they both placed their order. Once she stepped away, Ian looked up at Kade and broached the subject he'd come to him about.

"When was the last time you saw Alexandra?"

CHAPTER FIVE

Samantha shoved a donut in her mouth, her hair blowing in the breeze as they sat in the outdoor café. She looked more tense than Jillian had seen her in ages and furled her eyebrows in worry. Their normal Saturday morning breakfast routine usually helped them catch up on the week, but after the party the last weekend, along with Samantha and Kade's sudden exit, the tension was thick.

Jillian casually rolled her cell phone around her hand in a nervous habit. She couldn't believe she'd been so forward and asked a guy out. In a modern era it was 'normal,' and the feminist part of her was screaming from the rooftops, but she still felt uneasy about the whole concept. She looked down, checked the phone again, and frowned.

"You need to find a man who can take you in hand, throw you on your knees and demand your obedience while wooing you and treating you like a goddess," Samantha said between bites.

"Isn't that entire statement an oxymoron?"

Silence fell around them. It was exactly what Jillian craved, but what she often found was an either/or, not a both/and situation.

"It sounds great in theory, but all I keep seeing are the stacking failures. Guys usually just walk away, mumbling something about how I'm a great girl but..." Jillian forced a fake laugh to cover the hurt.

"It means they aren't good enough for you. It is the special combination you need." Samantha's hand covered Jillian's. "Your job isn't to make others happy. It is to know you are enough, no matter what happens."

"How's the PR business?" Jillian asked, trying to change the subject.

Samantha shrugged. "It's hard right now."

"Really? Why? You are great at it. Finding all the nooks and crannies to get people in and out of trouble. Finding all of their skeletons and dark closets."

"Yeah. I guess. I don't seem to do it well right now." She stared off into the distance.

"Why do you say that?"

"Because it's true." A look of sadness crossed her face and Jillian frowned.

"What aren't you telling me and how can I help?"

Samantha sighed.

"Atlas is missing." The words came out in a rush. "She left her phone, computer... everything behind. A sizable sum of cash was removed from her accounts. It's like she stepped off the Earth into nothing."

"Do you think it is foul play?"

"I don't know. I know something wasn't going right with her before it happened, but she was so tight-lipped about it."

This time it was Jillian's turn to comfort her friend. "You'll find her. I'm sure she'll pop up in the most unexpected places. Some old haunt she thinks everyone has forgotten about and poof, there she'll be, right as rain."

"You're a genius! Why didn't I think of something so simplistic?" Samantha beamed.

"What did I say?"

"The perfect combination of words. I know where she might be hiding. I don't know why."

Jillian looked confused but smiled at her friend's obvious epiphany. "That's great... I think."

Samantha nodded, pulled out her phone, and dialed. Across the table Jillian, could hear it ringing.

"Kade. I think I might have an outstanding idea where she's at..." Samantha spoke quickly into the phone. "No... no... not specifically, but I never checked out her old haunts.... She'd never go there... Well, could you check Boston?... Thanks."

She pushed the screen to disconnect the phone and turned back toward Jillian. "Now, what did you think of Ian?"

"Um... he was nice, just didn't seem to be interested in me. Still. I took the leap and asked him if he wanted to have coffee or something."

"Wow. Way to jump off the ledge. That's great. Where are you going?"

"Pump and Grind."

"Okay. Interesting first choice."

"I wasn't thinking about the name. It's a great coffee and bar combination."

"Maybe not consciously, but I think your subconscious wants you to get laid."

CHAPTER SIX

Ian walked into the trendy coffee shop and bar. His suit was rumpled from a long workday, making him wish he'd had a little more time to prepare rather than running late from a meeting. Across the room, he spotted Jillian perusing the upscale artsy menu.

"May I join you?" he asked as he approached her table.

"Um... yes, please."

"I'm sorry I'm late. My last meeting ran late."

"I saw your text. Thanks for letting me know."

He watched her fidget with the menu and avoid his gaze. Everything about her was interesting, but he knew they probably wouldn't match up. His tastes ran to the desires to have full control of a woman. To train her body to respond to him from a single word or a mere touch, but she didn't seem to be the type to give control to anyone. Still, everything about her made him crave those things like a man in the desert dying for a drink. The urges he got when he was around her were anything but gentlemanly.

The server came by and took Ian's order. When he looked up, their gazes met, and she smiled shyly, looked down at the table in front of her, and forced her eyes back up.

A thrill ran through Ian. He pretended for just a moment the reaction was because of him and his effect on her.

Ian had spend the day trying to concentrate on work, but his thoughts kept running to Jillian. He had to admit he wanted her. He'd caught himself checking his phone more often, hoping she might text him, but she had sent nothing else. It was odd that the behavior had done nothing to dampen his attraction. Instead it seemed to turn him on more. Whether it was because she'd asked him out, or his constant wayward thoughts of having his way with her. All day she'd lurked right on the edge of his mind, making it nearly impossible to concentrate on work.

The drinks were set down on the table between them and Ian startled out of his thoughts. He noted the small coffee stout in front of Jillian, and watched her pick it up, savoring the taste. It spoke of her enjoyment in the savoring the small things in life.

Their fingers touched as they both reached for a napkin. The electricity it sent through his body made him flinch and he looked up into her gaze as a visible shiver passed through her. For a moment their gazes held before she slid hers away demurely, tilting her head slightly and exposing her neck without artifice.

Fuck, Ian thought to himself. *Would it be so bad if I dragged her back to my place and found out what makes her squirm?*

"I'm hope you didn't think it too forward of me to ask you to coffee," she said, a blush running across her face.

Ian smiled.

"It was actually rather refreshing. There aren't many women who would ask a man out to coffee. How long have you been a member of the club?"

"I'm not. I was just Samantha's plus one the other night. She's been begging me for months to go with her, but I'm not much of a public player, so I didn't see the point."

"So you're new to the scene?"

"It depends on your point of view."

"And what is yours?"

"I'm new enough to still enjoy the edge and not new enough to be stupid."

Ian smiled at her quick reply. "What do you like best?"

She looked up and Ian saw mischief in her eyes. "Depends on the day."

"Oh? And what does today look like?"

"Like it would take quite a man," she said, smiling enigmatically.

"Now that sounds like a challenge." He narrowed his eyes speculatively as he studied her.

Jillian's mouth opened and closed several times, her glare communicating the thoughts as they ran through her head. Finally, she shut her mouth and pulled her eyes from his. She'd gone from ballsy to embarrassed in the span of a minute.

"I'm sorry. Almost. I don't know what's wrong with me. I know what I want, but I don't know that it actually exists. It's like this internal war. When a man says I'm a challenge, part of me wants to prove him right in all sorts of ways, and part of me wants him to win. Growing up, I learned early that submission to anyone meant failure and weakness, and success meant you had to always be strong and independent, no matter the situation. No one respects a woman who willingly submits to anyone and doesn't win in all challenges."

Ian nodded. "Most submissives seem to struggle with those ideas. The fine balance of being fiercely independent and yet curbing the need to run or fight when the opportunities are safe to do it. A place of equity in a perfectly inequitable exchange of power."

Her forehead furrowed and released as the emotions rolled across her face. It bothered him that he could do nothing to fix her internal strife, but he also knew it was a situation she'd battle on her own and come out the other side better for it. As he watched her silently struggle, she noticed his focused attention.

"What?"

He pressed a finger across her lips. "Shhh. I'm mind reading."

Jillian pushed his hand away and laughed. A growl threatened to rumble up from his depths, but he shoved it away. *Think normal interactions and thoughts.*

"Well, your thoughts are pretty easy to read. You wouldn't normally let a girl of yours get away with pushing your hand away that way."

"Not if she was mine."

"What would you do to her?"

"Remind her of her place." Ian leaned in close and whispered, "I'd bend her over my knee, discuss how much strength it took to have the self-control to want to submit in a world that screamed exactly the opposite. Then I'd make her count until I was sure she'd learned the lesson. When I was done, I would let her body slide from my lap and tell her how wonderful she was in her strength and how beautiful I found her desire to submit."

Her breath became deeply hypnotic as he watched her reaction with interest. He could see her desire for submission running just below the surface, right under her worldly armor. It was close but also fleeting. Still, he was sure he could draw it out of her with little effort. Everything in him wanted to test his hypothesis; his desire to push her and see what she would take made him almost instantly hard.

Jillian blinked hard, came back to the awareness of her surroundings, and took a long pull of her stout.

"Quite the interesting concept."

The snap back to business mode was so quick he would have doubted the previous moment had he not witnessed it.

"Have you ever filled out a checklist?"

"On my preferences? It's been years. I've known about the scene for a good while. Dabbled my toes in it, skirted the edges, played in private."

"Why don't I come by this week and we can take a look at one?"

She nodded.

"That would be interesting. Most people seem to just want to jump in on the action and if it fits well, then great and if not, they move on. It's never been a situation I've been overly comfortable doing."

"It's better to see where people are compatible," he started then leaned forward and narrowed his eyes slightly, giving her a stern look. "You have to be honest in your feedback or it won't work."

A glint of mischief reached her eyes. "Yes, Sir."

He chuckled at her cheeky reply. "I think you have a hard time being a good girl. You seem to enjoy mischief-making far too much."

She mirrored his actions, leaning toward him. Her scent drove him crazy. "No one seems to want to make me be good, so where's the fun in doing it?"

You have no idea what I'd like to do to you and how I'd show you how to behave.

Ian struggled to look indifferent. "If you're worried you can't mind your behavior, I can help you remember how to be good." The challenge in his voice brought a rise out of her and a smile quirked on the edge of his mouth.

"I'm not so sure about it. Many have tried and failed. What makes you think you're up to the challenge? You seem too nice and too helpful. Maybe the tables will turn in some unexpected ways and you'll beg to kneel at my feet."

"That sassy mouth could get you into some major trouble brat," he growled.

"Brat? It takes one to know one."

"More, it takes a brat tamer to understand a brat, and a firm hand to bring one inline. I could teach you to behave."

Jillian ducked her head slightly, her cheeks flushed. He fought the urge to take her in his arms and disarm her further with a searing kiss.

CHAPTER SEVEN

"Brats need to be taken in hand and taught there are those who can make them behave. I can see it's been a long time since anyone gave you structure, except yourself." His baritone voice fills her dream.

A smirk crosses Jillian's face. "It has only happened when I've chosen to let it happen."

Still, she takes a step backwards, away from his intense, challenging stare. There's something different about this one, but then she knows she's been wrong in the past. The windowless room now seems like a terrible idea as he stalks toward her. He is faceless.

With a slow shuffle, she moves backward with each step of his advance. Everything in her wants to stand her ground, but the tiny voice in the back is screaming to give in this once.

The backs of Jillian's knees hit the bed, and she forces them to straighten as they buckle.

"Bend over the bed."

The command is unmistakable, firm but soft. There is no reason for him to yell or scream; he knows she will comply. Her entire body shakes as she turns and gazes down at the red bedspread. His hands move over her body, lighting up every nerve.

I refuse to give in, she chants to herself.

"You'll only make it harder on yourself." His tone is a warning, and still the internal war rages, both applauding the bravado and hating the denial of needs.

He grabs her shoulders and shoves her forward. Her balance lost, Jillian tumbles forward. His hand wraps around the back of her neck, forcing her down.

"Discipline," he says, "is the practice of training people to obey rules or a code of behavior, using punishment to correct disobedience. It is a concept you will become well acquainted based on what I've seen so far. Also a branch of knowledge, one studied in higher education--and my dear, you need a higher education."

She shivers at his words. She hates them. She loves them. She fears them. She needs them. But they are just words-always just words.

His breath brushes against her ear. "As you know, manners maketh the man, or in this case a girl who's been free ranging for far too long."

His body straightens behind her. The cane whistles through the air.

Jillian screamed before it connected, sitting straight up in bed. Disoriented, she wondered what had just happened. A whimper escaped her mouth as the scream echoed against the wall. Her eyes wide with fear, adrenaline pumped through her veins. She felt his breath on her neck, the sweat on her forehead dripping down her cheek.

Her body sat shaking while her mind slowly dissolved the dream. The reality of her bed made her realize her true situation.

What the hell was that?

With an effort, her breath returned to normal from the intense dream. Between her legs, her soaked panties reminded her of her body's reaction, and her clit throbbed in its need for attention.

Glancing over at the clock, she mumbled. Ian was dropping by in thirty minutes and she needed to shower and dress. Jillian squeezed her legs together to stop the incessant throbbing, but it only increased the tempo.

She moaned.

With a sigh, she glanced at the clock and headed to the shower. The water ran in rivers down her body as she snaked her hand down until it reached between her legs. Her eyes closed and her mind pushed her to continue the scene that had startled her awake. Her fingers pushed through her folds and found her throbbing clit.

The faceless man is replaced with Ian. His suit crisp. A stern look across his face tells her he means business. He stretches out and crooks a finger toward her. She glides toward him and kneels when he points to the floor.

His stern stare makes her feel helpless under its weight. She would do anything to feel his pleasure again.

A moan slipped out of her mouth, as the images of her fantasy formed once against behind her closed eyelids, and bounced around the tile. She swirled a finger deep into her wetness and circled her clit in an attempt to satisfy her need.

Her fantasy Ian grabs her head, forcing her to look up into his harsh gaze. "So, brat. What do you have to say for your behavior?"

She knows she is in for a heavy punishment and also knows she deserves all of it. "Please..." she begs, "I'm sorry."

"You most definitely will be sorry when I'm done with you."

"Please, Sir."

"You wanted to be taken in hand. You need to be taken into hand. Now, come."

The words crossed her mind at the exact moment her fingers slid across her clit. The heat rushed to her pussy, her drenched fingers making it easy to move.

Ian pulls her across his legs. His lubed fingers play with the pucker of her ass. "I think keeping you full will remind you of your place. Right after I make this beautiful ass so red it will be difficult to sit for a couple of days without flinching."

Jillian slipped two fingers inside, her thumb caressing her clit. In her mind she could hear the lecture, but she didn't want a spanking. She also knew she would beg and promise to be better, but he would force her down.

She was on the edge of the most intense orgasm she'd felt in months. Two more quick strokes and she'd tumble into the bliss. Her thumb circled her clit.

The doorbell chimed across the intercom speaker. "Jillian. It's Ian."

"Damn it," she muttered to herself. Panicked, she grabbed a towel and pushed the call button for the door.

"Hey there." She tried to sound casual, but it came out in a breathy whisper. "I was in the shower. Give me a minute and I'll be right there."

Panic shot through her as she quickly dried off and ran into the bedroom, grabbing a pair of jeans and a T-shirt. She looked in her top drawer for underwear and realized her laundry was the chore of the day.

"Guess this meeting will be casually commando."

She sighed and looked up at the ceiling as if asking for help. When none came, she rushed to the bathroom, pulled a brush through her hair and walked to the front door.

She plastered on a fake smile, took a deep breath, and opened the door. "Sorry to make you wait. I lost track of time."

His suit looked just like the one in her dream, and her clit pulsated in response to the memory. Her nipples grew hard, and she flushed when she looked up.

Ian's eyes narrowed. Each movement seemed to study her with precision, and she was sure he knew what she'd been doing. His eyes glanced down to her chest, and he smiled.

"Nice to see you again," he said, mouth quirking at her obvious discomfort.

Her arms came up and covered her chest. "You too. Come on it. I need to go grab another shirt."

"Don't change on my account."

Jillian smiled. "Make yourself comfortable. I'll be right back."

Once in her bedroom, Jillian grabbed a bra, lifted off her shirt, and did a take two on the whole concept of dressing. The entire image of Ian standing in her doorway wearing an immaculate suit had done nothing to lessen the call of her needy clit between her legs. She didn't even need to look in the mirror to know it was obvious what was going through her mind when he'd arrived. With a deep breath, she tried to compose herself and headed back to the living room.

As she rounded the corner, she caught the sight of Ian looking at the painting above her fireplace.

"Everything okay, Jillian?"

The way he said her name made her knees almost buckle.

"Everything's fine. Why do you ask?"

"You seem... edgy, so to speak." He turned toward her and the smirk across his face told her he knew what she'd been doing when he arrived and the fact she'd been unable to complete the task at hand.

"I was in the middle of something when you arrived. It's no big deal."

"If now is a bad time, I can drop by when it is more convenient." He turned fully toward her, his face clouded in a tinge of worry.

"Now is fine. It's just been a long day." She rolled her neck for effect. "The artist is from the club."

"Excuse me?" Ian looked at her, confused.

"The painting you were admiring when I came in. It is by the house artist at the club."

"You mean Parker? The artist who does the club's human art shows?"

"One and the same."

"I didn't realize he did paintings." He looked at the other two paintings in a similar style across the room. "How do you know him? You said you weren't a member of the club."

"Parker and I went to college together. Periodically I'd pose for him and he'd create more interesting paintings."

"A nude model. How unexpected."

"A girl's got to pay the rent. Ramen noodles don't buy themselves, you know." Jillian smiled. Her mind wondered what it would be like to model for Ian. To be the sculpture, he'd want to mold.

"Too bad you kept none of them."

"They are on the back."

He cocked his head to one side and regarded her for a moment. Jillian walked over to the painting. As she reached for the frame, her hand brushed against his arm and sent a bolt of electricity from the contact. She turned over the frame and blushed inexplicably.

The nude body was wrapped in natural rope. Around her eyes lay a blindfold of wide black cloth. In her mouth sat three small kumquats on a skewer, a small ribbon securing it to the back of her head while small drops of drool pooled around the edge of her mouth.

"It's stunning."

"Thank you," she said, turning the frame back to its more mundane painting.

"Whose idea was it to double frame the two paintings?"

"Parker's. He loves the fact it hides in plain sight. Like so many of the things people do. Right underneath the surface they are not what they seem, but if you get a little closer and flip them over, you see a whole new view."

Ian's gaze swept across her body. "And what a view it would be too."

"Would you like a drink?" Jillian forced out as she turned toward the kitchen.

"Ice water would be nice."

She nodded and rushed into the kitchen. Would it be horrible if she dumped ice down her pants to curb the insistent need she found there?

CHAPTER EIGHT

Jillian walked back into the living room with the drinks. With each step she tried to calm her breathing, but it only made her body more aware of her heightened state. She stepped back into the room and handed him the glass. Goose bumps crawled up her arm as their fingers touched and she worked not to draw her hand back too quickly.

"Everything okay?" Ian asked.

He looked as if he would either eat her whole or he could read every secret she held.

"Great, why?"

"You seem... tense." His eyes danced with mischief. "Shall we sit?"

He waved his hand toward the couch.

She nodded and sat on the chair while he gracefully folded his body onto the couch across from her. "You don't have to sit so far away. I only bite a little."

"Oh, I'm sure you could play the wolf in many stories." She smirked.

He chuckled. "I only chase prey that wants to be chased. It's no fun otherwise."

Her mouth fell open and immediately she closed it. Could he possibly have figured out what she'd been doing when he'd arrived? Or that every time she looked into those eyes she wanted to melt and find out what it would be like to be his prey?

"I'm sure prey is easy for you to find." She smiled.

Part of her hoped he'd rise to the challenge while the other part wanted to chalk him up to being all talk.

He arched his brow.

"And do you know what I do with the prey I catch?"

"Play with them and discard them like most predators?"

"Be glad you're not my prey to find out," he said. His expression was unreadable as he took a sip of his water.

"Why? Too hard for you to catch?" Jillian challenged.

There was something about him that piqued her curiosity. Would he be the strict type or would he come on strong, only to fizzle to nothing like so many before him?

"You don't want to play this game, Jillian."

The way he said her name captured her complete attention.

"And why not, Ian? Afraid you'd lose for the first time in your overly privileged life?"

He shrugged. "I don't think you'd bend well enough for my desires and I don't break my toys."

"I don't break easily."

"Then why did you sit over there instead of over here?"

He pointed to the spot on the couch beside him.

"Because it is more polite to sit across from someone to converse."

"Bullshit. You're scared." His lips curled in amusement to her reaction.

"You don't scare me."

"Then please join me."

He leaned forward, elbows on his knees, and studied her. The look in his eyes dared her to move.

"You are an incorrigible ass," Jillian replied.

"Possibly. And if you were mine, that would be strike one," Ian said with a stern look on his face.

"For calling it as I see it?"

"No. For saying it disrespectfully."

She watched him through a sideways look. "So if I said it respectfully then it would be okay?"

"There's no way to call someone an ass in a respectful manner."

Jillian laughed. "Of course there is. You can say almost anything with a tone of respect."

"Oh?" He looked doubtful.

"In your attempt to express a dominant demeanor in which to invoke the desired response you appear to be quite the tomfool."

Ian laughs out loud. "Tomfool? You're going with tomfool?"

She blushed.

"Most people wouldn't realize the context."

"Well played, Dr. Hart. It would still land you over my knee for disrespect but gain my amusement because if anyone needs to be taken in hand it would most definitely be someone with a creative mouth like yours. Brat indeed."

"I prefer fiercely independent and slightly challenging." She raised her chin. In her mind she could see him rolling up his dress sleeve while he commanded her to take her place over his knee.

She gave her head a hard shake and took a sip of water. "How did you know my name?"

For a long moment he stared at her. Did he feel as lustful and aroused as she did?

"Kade. It seemed only fitting since Samantha gave you mine."

Jillian nodded. "I see."

"Everything okay?"

"Yes. I'm just not one to be very open."

"I understand," he whispered.

Something about him made her want to trust him. Both Kade and Samantha had given him a good recommendation, and while she didn't know Kade, the fact he was the head of Security was a good endorsement.

"You stay in your head too much."

She blinked and looked up. His steady gaze offered her an anchor in her lust-filled mind.

"No, I don't."

He smiled.

"Bet you do. You overthink every move you make with plans and backup plans."

Jillian squirmed as hit far too close to a truth.

"Close your eyes." He stood and walked over behind her chair.

"Why?"

"Close them," he commanded.

She took a deep breath, let out a sigh, and let them fall closed.

"Follow my words. Take a deep breath and relax."

Jillian took another deep breath. The tension drained slightly as she exhaled.

"Feel. In your body. Feel the movement of your breath. Don't think about it. Just relax. Focus only on your breathing."

His scent surrounded her. There was something about his nearness and voice that calmed her fears. The warmth of his body radiated around her.

Against her ear, his fiery breath caressed her neck.

"Do you want to be prey, Jillian?"

Every instinct in her wanted to run. Something about him was hot and a bit dangerous. If she took the risk to step across this line, she knew she'd fall to his control.

Her breath quickened in response to the combination of lust and fear roiling through her. It was a heady feeling, and she nodded.

"I need the words. Just follow me. You can do it."

"Yes."

"Excellent."

The praise sent a jolt of joy through her.

"Imagine the prey's hair wrapped in my hand, to control your every movement."

"Yes," she said as the air rushed out of her mouth.

If she thought she'd been lustful and wanting before it was nothing compared to how his words stoked the fire to a raging inferno. She wanted to beg him to touch her. If he could make her want this much with simple words, she wasn't sure what would happen at his hand. Her body felt like it was being taken on a roller coaster ride.

"You want someone to take you in hand. Take charge of your pleasure and help you express your internal pain. To spank you and then tell you when you may or may not come."

Jillian's brain felt fuzzy. His voice called to everything she'd ever hidden away from the world, in the need to be strong. She tried to think, but her throbbing clit and soaked pussy had her entire attention.

"To be taken. Claimed. Explore all of your fantasies without hesitation."

Her body shuddered as long repressed images exploded across her mind.

"The mark of ownership on your body."

"I don't think... "

"You shouldn't," he said.

His lips pressed against hers and she startled then relaxed into him. A moan escaped against their softness. He tasted as wonderful as he smelled. With each movement he guided her until her body released the tension under him. Then he took over the kiss, forcing her to open to him, daring her to fight what her body craved.

He moaned against her lips and she smiled in satisfaction, knowing she had an effect on him.

With reluctance she pulled away. She needed to gain control of the situation. Powerful women didn't submit, no matter how hot the fantasy. She looked up into his eyes and he stared back like he dared her to run so he could chase her.

"I should have asked to do that, but your reactions to my words made me want to taste you."

They stared at each other, wrapped in a spell neither wanted to break.

"You smell wonderful when you are turned on."

She glanced down and smiled at the tent in his pants. "Looks like it had the same effect on you."

"You will always be challenging." He let out an exasperated growl.

"Who? Me?" She batted her eyelashes.

"You are driving me fucking crazy."

"Obviously," she said and glanced down his body again.

Part of her wanted to tease him without mercy and push him right to the edge, to see if the predator below the surface would actually chase her like prey. The control and discipline turned her on. Jillian wondered what it would be like to curl up in his arms after an intense scene with him or to feel his control to release both pain and pleasure. Her mind surfaced out of the cloud and screamed.

"Good thing I'm not submissive and thus not what you're looking for," she said, breaking the spell that held them.

The magic of the moment evaporated and for a long moment she wished she was exactly what he was looking for and the moment hadn't been broken.

He nodded, his face full of regret. "You will be a challenging handful for someone."

Jillian forced a smile. "So others tell me."

One thing was crystal clear to her: she couldn't let herself get swept away again. He'd just use her as fun prey and discard her when he'd finally captured her. Men like Ian didn't want for dates and she was sure women threw themselves to kneel at his feet.

Ian straightened and walked back to the couch. In mere seconds he was all business. "How about I set up a couple of meetings with other people in the club? You said you weren't sure what you wanted anymore. Maybe exploring possibilities might help you narrow it down."

She shrugged noncommittally. The last few relationships had not ended well, and she wasn't sure she was ready to go down the path again.

"You must let your guard down a little, though," he said, startling Jillian out of her thoughts.

"I don't know how to let it down anymore."

"Doesn't seem to be a problem with me. Even though you're scared of something, you still open."

Something inside her wanted to disagree, but even she knew it was true.

"It seems you want to put up a strong defense perimeter. You want to be strong and independent, but that doesn't have to change for the right person, you know. If you want a relationship with a version of a power dynamic, it can always be one of equal inequality. It's not always about me dom, you sub. Sub obey dom."

Jillian laughed.

"Who's saying I will not be the dominant in the relationship?"

While the words rolled off her tongue, her gut wanted to know what it would be like to submit to him. There was something safe about him. It made her want to curl up into him and let the world fade away. No matter how much she wanted to deny it.

"You wouldn't with me."

She looked down at the floor and inhaled.

"There's something about you that's just different. It's really too bad what you want is an intense submissive who will obey every command without question. I'm just not that kind of person. I've worked hard to have my own voice, my own life, and my own opinions. It might be fun to play at it periodically, but I don't know I could do it as an actual power exchange in life. No matter how wonderful it might be."

As soon as the words left her mouth, she wanted to take them back. She couldn't believe the things that had just tumbled out of her as he sat there. It felt like a moment of freedom, but she couldn't lose all the things she'd gained just for a moment with him. To pursue a relationship like this would only end in heartbreak.

"I won't apologize for what I am or what I'm looking for in a woman."

"Don't you like your women to think? Do you not want them to have a life outside of you?"

"It's not like that for me. To be intensely mine is about my ability to respect a woman. To protect her and the trust she freely gives. It is about control for mutual benefit and pleasure. No less is it about making pain tangent in the demand she takes it for me. I am a demanding dominant, but I give far more than I take to make a bond stronger than most relationships with more formal paper."

His words ran through her mind. Protection, trust, and pleasure pushed all her amazing fantasies through it. On the flip side, the concepts of pain and control prickled at her sense of self.

"It all sounds horrid and wonderful."

"Those are two words rarely put in the same sentence."

"Honestly, I get stuck on the ideas of pain and control. They make my skin crawl and go against everything in my life."

"Have you ever experienced something that challenges and pushes you to the edge? Once you get through it there's a rush of pleasure?"

"No. Not really. I've had moments of satisfaction when I've finished a project or accomplished a goal, but nothing so astounding as to be life-changing."

"It sounds like it has potential on paper but the reality... I don't know."

"Why don't you let me show you what it is like and you can see if it is on your list or not? Though I will warn you, I'm not an overly tolerant dominant. I'm exacting in my desires and my commands."

"So follow you or pay the price?"

"Yes, Jillian, that is how this all works. But you've been around the scene long enough to know it. You aren't some newbie fresh into this world. There's something about you that's jaded."

Her eyes lifted to see him watching her in a calculating stare. Would it be worth it to jump off the edge? To step into that world again just for a moment and submit? To live to his exacting standards and face punishment if she did not? The last time she'd stepped into such a situation the abuse had been overwhelming. For years she'd thought all power exchange relationships were nothing but covers for the domestic violence she'd experienced. It was only when she'd become a sex counselor did she understand the positives of an actual power exchange and the difference from abuse.

Maybe it was exactly what she needed to finally lay down the last pieces of her past to rest. She'd seen amazing couples and poly families come through her office, counseling them through the bumps in the road of alternate lifestyle arrangements. She'd always thought she'd end up in a basic romantic relationship with a little kinky fun on a rare occasion for spice and release. Yet here was a man offering her the one thing she feared.

"What are you offering then?" she finally asked.

"The basics. To allow you to train with me from the ground up."

"You want to treat me like a newbie?"

"I want to treat you as I would a new submissive in my care. To train you in the way, I prefer things, to show you that another person can be trusted and for us both to have fun. It seems like it might be exactly what you need."

"And what do you get out of it?"

Ian shrugged. "I enjoy the training. To watch another person bend and submit. When they choose to learn and change, it is a rush all its own."

For a long moment she waited for him to add more but realized he'd said all he was going to on the subject. At least she knew she would not be masturbation fodder for him. As if he could read her thoughts, his stare became heated. His body language changed as if the thoughts mirrored hers and he enjoyed the images passing through his mind.

For the next few hours the ease of their conversation helped them both relax more around one another. They laughed easily at the stories of each other's lives. With more comfort than she'd ever experienced, they discussed their various likes and dislikes with the kinky realm and more mundane hobbies. With an ever-increasing regularity, they found more similarities than differences and Jillian enjoyed the evening.

Ian glanced at his watch. "It's late."

Jillian yawned as if her body agreed with his assessment.

"You should get in bed. Let's meet up next Friday at the club. I'll put you on the list as a guest and we can use one of the private rooms for our first session together. There are more safety protocols there and I don't want you to feel pressured to do things. Consider it neutral ground."

"Sounds good."

She walked him to the door, and he leaned down, his lips a mere inch from hers. *Please kiss me*, her body shouted.

"Anticipation of what you desire is a marvelous thing," he said and planted a kiss on her forehead.

A frown marred her face slightly, and she watched a smile curl on his lips.

"That's just mean."

"It's only the beginning, my dear."

From the windows she watched him drive away, then climbed into bed and finished what she'd started earlier. This time the fantasy slammed into her mind, mixing with his smell, the feel of his lips, the stern look on his face. The orgasm caught her off-guard as it slammed into her body. Waves of pleasure rolled through her while her body spasmed and climbed to a second orgasm. Within seconds, another wave took her to the edge and threw her over the abyss into a pleasure-filled sleep.

CHAPTER NINE

Kade puffed on the cigar. He looked more tense than Ian had ever seen him. Since the moment he'd found out Kade's best friend and former dominant had disappeared under unusual circumstances, he'd watched his friend close up to the rest of the world.

Ian reached for his glass of rum and lifted it to his lips. The news from the field was not good, but so far the trail was still warm enough his team didn't suspect foul play.

"The last thing the team found, after she withdrew a sizable sum of money, was a movement toward the northeast."

With a nod, Kade sat in silence.

"What are you not telling me?" He stared at his friend for a long moment.

"I suspect she was hiding something from me when she left."

"Why do you think she left?"

"There was something about the way her things were placed on the desk. Too perfectly to be in a hurry or to have struggled. It was like she wanted to tell me something, but couldn't bring herself to do it. I feel like I've failed her."

"You didn't fail her, Kade. You can't protect people who don't let you in."

"See, that's the thing. I'm just security. The friend. A few months ago she dated a guy I knew from the military. Everything was going so well between them. I'd never seen her so happy. Then overnight it all blew apart."

"Why?" Ian probed. Every piece of information he could feed his team would help them find her.

"She didn't let him in to her world and when it all blew up, it almost cost his sister a Congressional seat."

"Wait." Ian sat up in his chair. "Are you telling me Atlas didn't tell someone she dated that she was also Alexandra, the dominatrix and club owner?"

Silence fell between them for a long moment. Ian could tell Kade struggled with the decision about how much to divulge. Finally he nodded.

Ian let out a low whistle. "Now that's a hell of a bombshell to find out through the media. So she was his dominant, and he didn't know he was sharing her?"

"That's the thing. She was submissive to him."

"This one keeps getting better." Ian shook his head.

"I tried to tell her the only way for the dynamic to work was honesty. She knows that -- it's one of the things she drills into her people. I think in her mind the two were almost separate things. She was good at both jobs, but in some ways they were two different lives and she spoke of them like two different people. It never made much sense to me, but I wanted to give her room even when it didn't always seem logical."

"People aren't always rational creatures."

"Don't I know it," Kade said and took a long draw on the cigar. Smoke billowed from his lips when he sighed.

"I think she was being stalked."

Ian quirked an eyebrow. While it wasn't unheard of for a professional dominatrix to be stalked by her clients, Atlas/Alexandra had one of the best security teams he knew.

"What makes you think she's being stalked? Do you have evidence?"

"Right before she disappeared, she blew off her security team. The level of her secrecy increased, and every time I approached her on it, I swear I could see the fear in her eyes before she closed up on me."

"It's not unusual for clients to push security away if they are being blackmailed or stalked. There's something about those situations that makes them think if they follow along, the person will just go away."

"Yeah. I can't believe I missed the signs and didn't push her harder to open." Kade ran a hand over his face in frustration.

"You can only protect people who want to be protected."

Kade nodded, lost in thoughts far too dark.

"We'll find her." Ian put his hand on his friend's shoulder.

"I know. It's why I brought it to you. Samantha has been scouring the inter-webs for a hit. The fact Atlas has been using cash works against us."

"She's smart. It'll be okay."

"Too smart. That woman needs to be taken over someone's knee when this is all said and done. Reece, the guy she was seeing, is beside himself in rage and worry. He screamed at her right before she disappeared. It was ugly. He's blaming himself for it, but also wants to spank her until she can't sit down for months for making everyone worry."

"Now that sounds like a man in love."

"Indeed. Just don't tell him."

They both chuckled at the joke.

"I'm glad you can still smile, even through this one."

Kade stared at his glass a minute and looked up as if trying to force his mind to change subjects.

"So, I hear you got a room downstairs for you and a girl name Jillian."

"Yeah. She's the girl you had me save at the bar the other week."

"The one Samantha had tried to push Evan onto?"

"The same. One of those fiery independent types."

"Are you exploring submission now, Ian?" Kade grinned.

Ian laughed. "Been there, done that, but you liked it more than I do."

Kade chuckled.

"She wanted to explore a little, and I thought it would be a fun side project for now."

"Ian the Brat Tamer," Kade said, mimicking the crack of a whip.

CHAPTER TEN

Ian checked his watch again and turned to pace the room. Either she was one of those who disrespected others with her lateness or she wasn't coming. The time they'd agreed upon had come and gone over twenty minutes ago. His hard-on had nagged him all day. It seemed other than the discussion he'd had with Kade, her image consumed his thoughts.

It made no sense to get excited about a short-term project. She wasn't what he was looking for, and he was too intense for her. Sure, he wanted to play with her, but the offer to give her a taste of training seemed insane now.

He'd tried to force himself to sit down in the enormous studio room; instead he'd paced to relieve the building tension. Across the room he caught his image in the wall of mirrors. Around the room stood various pieces of equipment and he could easily imagine Jillian in every position.

The entrance door to the room creaked open. His body straightened as he stared in the mirror watching the reflection of the room. When the door opened fully, Jillian stood in the door, her eyes wide with trepidation.

"You're late."

She cautiously stepped into the room. "I know. I... I'm sorry."

She could tell she was trying to appear more confident than she felt as she straightened her body.

"Why are you late?" His voice was stern, and he continued to watch her in the mirror, not even turning to face her.

"I could tell you it was traffic, but it would be dishonest." Jillian chewed on her lower lip. "This scares me. Last night brought no sleep. Then I thought how stupid it was to feel scared. It's not like I haven't done these things before." She lifted her hand to sweep it around the room but dropped it, her eyes dropping with it. "It's just... there's so much... I don't know."

He heard her voice quaver through the last few words. "Come here."

Ian felt like an ass but also knew head games were easy to play. Too many times he'd had submissives work his emotions for leniency, consistently taking subtle control while crying fowl if he didn't control them enough when they wanted something. He watched her reflection. It took guts to show up over twenty minutes late, especially when she'd been in the scene for several years.

"Take off your shoes, place them by the door, and pour us both a glass of water."

She quirked a brow at him and he watched a challenging look float across her face, but without a word she complied. Her skirt clung sinfully to her ass as she walked across the room. His gaze continued to follow her while he walked over to the table and sat down. With two glasses of water in her hands, Jillian walked over to join him.

"Please sit. We should go over the paperwork before we go any further. I printed out the checklist and emails you sent me so we could discuss them."

"I see," she said, and he wished he could read her thoughts.

No longer the relaxed person he'd kept up far too late the other night, today she was all business and a bundle of tension, as she sat down across from him.

Ian scanned the papers in his hands, pretending to put thought into them. Although he'd already read them multiple times earlier in the day, he enjoyed watching her squirm across from him. It set a respectful tone, especially since she'd arrived so late.

Most of their interests matched. A few of his more intense desires were on her soft limit list but he wasn't surprised at her hard limits. He noted that most of the pain activities did not reach her soft limit list but rated low on desirability. When he reached the area concerning the bodily contact, it had surprised him to find it had included sex. Reading it again now added to his already aroused state.

Focus, he commanded himself. *Don't look like a horn dog or some teenage boy who only thinks with his dick.*

"Let's talk about your list."

"There's not much to talk about," she quickly countered. "It's a standard checklist. Either our kinks line up or they don't."

"Stop," Ian admonished. "You know how important communication is for this situation to work. If you were new to it all, I'd cut you some slack, but you aren't. Just so you know, our kinks line up extremely well, a little too well." He paused and let the weight of his words hand in the air. "For your safety, you should know this room contains several cameras for security reasons. You can choose to have the cameras on so security can monitor the room and give you a second layer of safety, or you can turn them off."

"The camera can be off. I don't know that I want security to see what is going on in here. I know they are used to it, and I appreciate the extra security."

Silence hung in the air. He watched her body language change from defensive to a slow, more open compliance, but still she held her challenging air.

"Now let's discuss why you were late."

The bravado she'd built over the last few minutes deflated at the mention of her tardiness. "I have no excuse. This entire idea makes me nervous, but I should have either been on time or informed you of my probable tardiness."

"Correct. Yet you chose neither of those scenarios. Why? Were you trying to play games and test my patience from the outset? I'm strict on my expectations, more so because you knew better than the choice you made today."

"I'm sorry I disrespected you, Sir."

The word crossing her lips went straight to his groin and he bit back a groan.

"Is it the idea of punishment that drove you to an irrational decision? To see if you would get punished for willfully being late?"

"Pain scares me."

"Yet you placed yourself, knowingly, in a position of punishment from the start. Already challenging me to see if I would follow through? Do you want to walk this path, Jillian?"

She licked her lips nervously. "Yes."

"Are you sure? Because willful disobedience just to push my buttons will end our arrangement as quickly as it started."

"I'm sure, Sir."

"There's no reason for honorifics. Our arrangement is a temporary dynamic to allow you explore control and submission."

"How would you like to be addressed?"

"Ian is fine."

"As you wish, Ian."

The turn of phrase made him think of a genie in a lamp and in the same moment just as much of an honorific as the word Sir. He suppressed the shudder that ran through his body.

"What is your safe word?"

"The ones used as standard by the club."

"Stop light words it is then. Kneel," he said, pointing to the floor beside his chair.

With only a slight hesitation, she stood, walked to his side, and folded herself into a kneeling position. The grace of her movement spoke of position training. She knelt with her legs together, hands down on her thighs and back straight. Her eyes looked forward and slightly down. The position was reminiscent of his time in Japan and the various formal ceremonies he'd both participated in and observed.

He could tell it had been some time since she'd practiced, but there was a beauty in her subtle movements. There was a mixture of self-consciousness mixed with a personal pride.

When she settled into the position, a change coursed through her body, almost as if something in her recognized it as being home. Yet the slight tilt of her head held a challenge.

"You've had positional training."

"Yes." Her curt voice sat in opposition to the relaxed nature of her position.

Ian reached down and took a hold of her jaw and waited. The muscles in her body rotated through tension to relaxation in waves as he held her firm. He watched the internal war in the subtle changes across her face and could almost hear the argument between handing him control and challenging him until he gave up. His hand increased the pressure until she went docile and he watched a wash of peace flow across her face. It stirred every possessive and protective need in him. Someone had hurt her deep enough to make her push the world away in fear. He let his fingertips brush against her cheek, unable to resist the intimate gesture of assurance. Her eyes closed and her cheek fell against his hand. When he withdrew it, a whimper escaped her lips.

Jillian eyes opened. They were soft and bottomless as if all cares had melted from her. Just as quickly, they gained their normal alertness, and he watched her body tense once again.

"I can be both hard and soft. Challenging is never a good move, especially when it is irrational and emotional." He slid his hand down her shoulders and back up the side of her neck. Once again her eyes fluttered shut and her body relaxed with a deep breath. "In this place the world vanishes. Are you remembering how this place feels?"

"Yes," she breathed.

"You should allow yourself to fall into it more often. Soft and compliant."

Her eyelids snapped open and she glared at him. "Compliant? You want me soft and compliant so it is easy to run all over me..."

Before she could complete the sentence, he buried his fist into her hair. Jillian gasped at the sudden move but did not pull away. He watched her eyes lose focus again, and she relaxed back into the position at his feet. His fist tightened, and she moaned.

He leaned down, his lips barely away from her ear. "If you keep challenging me, you'll get in deeper than you'd asked to go."

Ian lifted his hand and traced her lips with his fingers. She opened her mouth and yielded to his touch. He adjusted the grip in her hair and she whimpered. Tentatively her tongue darted out and met his finger. His touch replied by pushing it into her mouth and her lips closed around it, sucking him gently. Between his legs, his cock jumped as he imagined her lips around him. He pulled his finger from her mouth.

"Strip."

Jillian's eyes opened, and she started to say something, but he placed his finger across her lips.

"I didn't ask for your intellectual opinion on the subject. I gave an order and I expect it to be followed without question. There was nothing in your paperwork which indicated a naked body to be a hard limit. This isn't a discussion. It is a lesson in trust."

Behind his finger, her mouth closed, and he watched her eyes fall.

"Now let's try this again. Strip."

He watched her hesitate again. Then her body unfolded into a standing movement with the grace of a dancer rising on her toes. A breath shuttered through her as she stood beside him. With an air of reluctance, she stepped around him in slow, deliberate movements. Ian knew it was a combination of internal challenges and a slight stall to avoid the inevitable. Her eyes scanned the floor as her fingers wrapped around the zipper of her shirt.

"Eyes on me. Your eyes will always be on me when I give you a command unless I direct otherwise."

She nodded, and her eyes lifted to meet his.

"When is the last time you heard that order?"

His question must have caught her off-guard because she stopped in mid-movement; the shirt had just reached the bottom of her bra line. Ian took in a breath as she continued to move the shirt upward and over her head, then folded it neatly and placed it on the table before him. Immediately her fingers hooked into the waistband of her skirt.

"I asked you a question. Don't think just because you have a beautiful body that I am so easily distracted."

"My body is far from beautiful. I'm soft around the middle, my ass is huge, and I could really use some solid diet and exercise..."

"Did I ask for an opinion of your body?"

"No."

"Did I ask you another question?"

She nodded.

"Words. I want words."

"Yes. You asked me another question."

"And here you are willfully avoiding the question."

Her eyes once again fell to the floor avoiding his gaze.

"Eyes up."

His heart beat hard against his chest, and he hoped she couldn't hear the effect she was having on him. Every movement, every challenge and every moment of obedience pushed every dominant button in him.

"Now answer the question. When was the last time you heard the order to strip?"

Jillian's chest rose and fell as she took a deep breath. "Seven years ago."

There was something in the way her voice tightened at the memory that made him want to call a halt to the situation. Her eyes rose once again to meet his. In their depths he could see the need to know she was safe, and he would challenge her just as much as she was pushing him.

"I didn't tell you to stop. You can talk and remove clothes at the same time."

A whimper escaped her, but she continued to remove each article of clothing and fold it neatly on the table. Inch by inch, she bared herself to him. Her eyes periodically fluttered away from his gaze, only to return with significant effort when she forced herself to comply. Ian adjusted himself through his pants as her body came into view.

When all of her clothes were piled on the table before him, he sat in the room's quietness and watched her. Jillian's hands twitched by her sides, periodically pulling forward to cover herself, then return alongside her hips. Seven years might have passed since she'd been in this position, but she knew the expectations, no matter how much she fought herself.

"Kneel," he commanded, pointing to the spot between his legs.

Once again he watched her fold herself gracefully into a closed kneeling position. When she settled, he grabbed her chin and lifted it upwards. "Your body is beautiful. We are going to get something clear right here and right now. Insulting your body will result in swift punishment. It is a direct insult to me."

"But it's my body..." she started.

"And your body is to my taste, so to insult it is to insult my taste in a woman's body and thus a direct insult to me."

He let the words settle around them. "I get the distinct impression you are used to getting your way and have only allowed yourself to experience situations in which you control the outcome. This is not one of those situations. If it is the situation you thought you were going to walk into today, then you have my permission to take your leave, but we will not play again. When we discussed the situation the other day, I offered to take you back to a place of not being in control."

Jillian struggled to keep his gaze and fidgeted between his knees.

"Am I boring you?"

Her eyes snapped up. "No, Ian."

"I'm not an overly patient person, Jillian. Is this the experience you seek?"

"Yes, Ian." The way she said his name made him want to groan at the way his body reacted.

"Now to address your tardiness, your reluctance and your challenging nature."

In one fluid motion, he reached down and moved her until she was dangling across his lap. He swatted her upturned ass six times, finding her wiggling and yelps both sexy and distracting. This was supposed to be correction. Forcefully, he placed her back in position and wrapped his hand in her hair and gave her a couple more swats. When he was done, he let the tips of his fingers trace across her body.

"Punishment is never the path you should choose. If you desire my attention, no matter the type, there are much better ways to get it. Remember that. You will always find it is better to express your desires than to ever try to manipulate the situation."

He could feel her pants and her body shake as he continued to caress her skin.

"So noted."

He let the indiscretion of her non-verbal answer pass and leaned back in the chair, her exposed body at his mercy. Music lilted through the room from the remote he'd picked up off the table in front of him. Jillian's body relaxed, and he pushed her back between his knees, as he ran his finger gently through her hair.

CHAPTER ELEVEN

Jillian tried to focus on the situation. Past moments of training floated in and out of her mind, his hand rhythmically taking her to a place of peace. Her body twinged in a vague discomfort. She'd just met this man and, outside of the recommendation of her dear friend, knew little about him. Yet here she was on her knees, kneeling naked and vulnerable and at more peace than she'd experienced in years.

His words about insulting her body floated to the forefront of her mind. She had no illusions about her appearance. There were so many other women who were more beautiful and stunning. With looks like his, he could easily have one of them in this position.

"You are beautiful, Jillian." His voiced rumbled through the room, startling her from her thoughts. His fingers ran down the side of her neck and instinctually she dropped her head to allow him access to her vulnerability.

"Such soft skin," he murmured, pushing his seat back to give him better access. Jillian adjusted her body to accommodate the loss of his but remained quiet. Everything in her wanted to argue, but she tried to hold on to the last moments of peace before her independent nature reared its ugly head at the feeling of being treated like property.

"Such poise and grace." He stood, moved his hand to his side, and pushed the chair way. Without a sound he stepped behind her. "What does a worship pose look like to you?"

She slipped one hand over the other and slid her body forward until her forehead touched the floor. The change eased the pressure on her legs but left her lower body open to his view.

"Very nice. Such a beautiful body."

The words hung in the air. She knew she should thank him for the compliment, but internally the war that ruined everything ignited.

"I believe you were given a compliment. What do you say when someone does so?"

"Thank you for the compliment, Ian, though my opinion on the subject are different."

The slap across her ass burned before the words finished crossing her lips.

Jillian let out a yelp and raised up, but his foot pushed gently across her neck, holding her in position. Across her skin, the burn dissipated in time for the second blow.

"While I enjoy an intelligent conversation and tête-à-tête, this is neither the time nor are you in a position for such."

She could hear the reproach in his voice; it was both comforting and lit her on fire in the same instance. In her mind, she promised him an earful when they were back on equal ground, but for now he'd made his point and she settled back into the position. The fire on her ass subsided and other parts of her body reacted to the awakening of areas she'd long since forced to be dormant.

"Very nice. I will follow through with my words. If I let something slide, do not think I did not notice it. Just like your earlier failure of proper address. Am I clear?"

"Yes Ian," she mumbled into the carpet.

"Let's try this again. You have a beautiful body, Jillian."

"Thank you, Ian."

"Good, an eager student after all." She could hear the smile in his voice. "Kneel up, eyes up."

Jillian pulled her body back to a kneel on her heels, then slowly propelled it upward until her weight was balanced on her knees, her lower legs on the floor for support. She watched Ian walk back in front of her and lifted her eyes to meet his. The slight jut of her jaw gave a silent moment of defiance, but she backed down when she met the stern expression on his face.

He went quiet. His eyes barely moved as he watched for each subtle movement of her body. Part of her wanted to stand up and end things right in this moment, but a bigger part of her wanted to prove to herself that her experience was not the norm. Her body tensed under his scrutiny. Was he testing her? Did he think she wasn't good enough for him or she would panic?

If he'd just let her drop her eyes from his gaze, she could block out this feeling and find the peace of being ignored. The voice in her head shouted she was weak and sick.

This is how the abuse started last time. You just gave in and submitted. He was right, you are worse than nothing. It's why they all walk away.

Jillian tried to push the words away. She'd worked too long and hard to get past the guilt of abuse and try the one relationship type she craved. Yet the first time she tried, her demons surrounded her.

"You fight yourself too much." His breath whispered against her ear and she startled. "If I wanted you in your head, then we'd be doing something far different." Ian pinched her nipple hard, and she gasped in a shocked breath.

Lightly he wiped away the tear she'd not realized had fallen and smiled down at her, as he pulled his body back to its full height. "Much better. Welcome back."

"When was the last time you had a release?"

She struggled to understand his words, or the context wanted. Jillian scowled in confusion.

"If my question was not clear, then you need to ask for clarification. Your words are what I need from here."

"What type of release?"

"Cathartic."

Her eyes dropped to the floor. The need for emotional release hung just under the surface. "Never."

Ian knelt down and cupped her chin, raising it until her eyes once again met his. "Why not?"

"I can't get past the pain. Most create releases through extensive amounts of pain."

"Will you allow me to try?"

A dozen conflicting thoughts coursed through her mind. She'd never been asked by her former dominant for anything; he did what he wanted to do. Fear and excitement raced side by side through her body. Her headed nodded.

"I need words, Jillian."

Jillian struggled. The need to vocalize her words was embarrassing and difficult.

"Yes Ian. Please try," she said, her voice strained and hoarse.

"If you want to stop, your safe words can halt everything immediately."

"Yes, Ian."

"Good. Rise and walk over to the bench." He held out his hand and helped her to her feet.

The well-appointed room drew her attention as she turned toward his gaze. Along one wall hung a large highly polished wooden X. The St. Andrew's cross was beautiful in its craftsmanship and simplicity. Two large cabinets lined the wall closest to the door. Pulled out from the wall sat the bench. Shaped in a triangle, two thin rails ran along either side with the center higher in the middle.

Jillian walked over to the waist-high bench and let her fingers run along the leather. She took a deep breath and moved her body into position. On either side she placed her knees on the rails, lay her body down the center and let her arms fall on the upper part of the padded rails. The blue leather felt cool to her skin, and she shivered.

"Comfortable?" Ian said, his voice low.

Looking over her shoulder, she nodded.

"This is your last warning, Jillian." His hand crashed against her ass and she yelped. Use... your... words."

"Yes, Ian."

"Are you ready to proceed?"

"Yes, Ian."

"Much better."

"Catharsis allows us to face that which we cannot make tangible." His voice took on a stern quality, each word an underlying command. "The idea of catharsis can draw both fear and hope to the surface in an internal battle. To begin a new relationship on solid ground, one must release the old. I am not a man who shares well with ghosts, and neither will any of your future prospects."

Ian placed his hand on her shoulder and moved it down her body.

"But you must also want to release," he continued. "To be cleansed. It is not a process of one encounter, rather it is a process where you move through the release of all of your emotions. It is meant to give you a place to face your anger, fear, sadness and hurt and equally open you to experience joy, hope, pleasure, and freedom. To separate them as individual concepts is foolish at best and it allows you to hold on to things which should be released, at worst."

Jillian shivered under his touch. The force of his words pushed her in ways she'd never experienced.

"Catharsis is not usually a first-encounter exercise, but I feel you need to experience it to help you figure out what you want in a relationship. There's something about you that needs to find release in both pleasure and pain, sadness and joy, fear and freedom, anger and love. To clean out the deepest, darkest recesses and purify yourself. If you find things become too much, just remember to use your words."

Jillian shivered under his touch. His words hit cords deep in her she'd long forgotten and things she no longer hoped to find.

"You are beautiful," he started, and she turned her head away from him. His hand came down swiftly across her ass cheeks, and she yelped as her body lifted off the bench.

"When we are done, you will accept the statement as true."

"I can't..."

"You will." The determination in his voice sent a frisson of energy down her spine.

So many times she'd heard how she wasn't enough. Her sassiness made her unwanted, or she wasn't the perfection of a cover magazine model. No matter how many hours she'd spend for Him, she was never graceful enough in her poses, never fast enough in her responses, never ready enough even when all he did was simply bent her over. Everything about her was ugly in her mind, and she couldn't fathom how to let go of it all for Ian or anyone else. She realized how much she wanted to follow him. There was something safe about him. He was both soft and hard, stern and caring. It was an oxymoron she couldn't wrap her mind around and now he demanded that she believe in her own beauty.

His hands ran over her body, each stroke alternating between a firm knead across her skin to a feather-light touch.

"Your body is beautiful. It is very responsive to touch. You shiver when you let go and allow your body to simply feel."

Every time his hands reached her ass, she tensed in readiness for a strike that didn't come. Lips replaced the trails where his fingers left their heat on her skin.

"You are beautiful in the way you move. Each movement planned before execution as if by hours of memory. The elegance and grace you exude are fascinating and lovely. You must have been the pride of all the men who've come before me."

It wasn't his touch that raked at her emotion, she realized, it was his words. Each one pushed against the wall she refused to open, as if checking for the key to the door she didn't remember installing.

"You want to please so much, to give all you are, and yet you hold back. It is a shame to see such beauty caged behind the wall built on the mistakes of men. Do you know how beautiful you are as you lie here under my touch?"

She shuttered at his words. Something in her uncurled.

Her body responded to his sensual touch as his words wormed their way through her mind. The softness of his fingers followed the warmth of his breath. Jillian relaxed under his touch as she let go of her control and accepted his words, or at least tried. With each moment became a little easier, and though she couldn't seem to fully open to him, she wanted to give him a chance.

"That's so beautiful. So very lovely." His hand trailed down her spine, along her ass cheek and grazed across her pussy lips.

A whimper escaped her throat, and she struggled not to push back toward his fingers. Her heart thundered in her chest. This was only supposed to be an experiment, a taste of possibilities. She let her mind follow the winding path of his words. To offer everything inside her and give it to him.

"Please," she whispered.

His fingers slid through her wetness. "So exquisite." Over and around her clit, his fingers moved, teasing her and then moving to other parts of her body. Only to return and torture her by tapping, rubbing, and pinching her clit.

Jillian moved under his touch. She shifted on the bench, trying to follow his fingers. Ian caught her clit between his fingers and pinched hard. She cried out against the leather.

"Are you beautiful?"

When she didn't answer, he pinched harder, and she squealed.

"I asked you a question, Jillian." The dark seduction of his voice threatened to push her over the edge as she struggled for words.

Ian didn't let up. His thumb rubbed over the sensitive bud, pushing her closer to the edge. She tried to fight back from the edge enough to form words, but her body teetered too close. As quickly as it started, his fingers stopped, her body squirmed with need and she cried out in frustration.

"Words. Use your words, Jillian."

"Maybe to you."

"Wrong answer," he said menacingly in her ear.

His hand slammed against her ass in quickly slaps. When he was done, his fingers stroked through her wetness and she was quickly reminded of how close she'd been when he stopped. Behind her, Ian sighed appreciatively. "Open for me, beautiful. Give me your pleasure. Release your pain."

The constant move between hard and soft left her spinning. Something deep inside her snapped with each new movement of his hand or slow radiant tone of his low seductive words. A loud moan escaped her lips, every muscle in her body strained right on the edge. She wanted more. Needed more.

"Give it to me, now."

The dam inside released as the orgasm took her over the edge with an unexpected force. Her body bucked, clenching on nothing, frustrated at the need for more of a release. Ian let up his ministrations until her body shivered in the aftershocks, then returned once more to teasing and torturing her clit.

She wanted to beg him to stop, she wanted to beg him not to stop. For over two years she'd not been in a steady relationship and her late-night fantasy sessions didn't hold a candle to his expertise. Orgasm shock waves pulsed through her, and he once again ramped her to another one. Over and over, he led her to the next peak until something in her body broke open on the crest of the fourth orgasm.

Tears welled in her eyes. One spilled over the edge. Then they came in an uncontrollable torrent as Ian pushed her through another orgasm. Pleasure turned into pain. She wanted to beg him to stop, but the sobs caught in her throat until she could not speak.

He pushed her until her orgasm shot through her in a searing white light her world went black.

JILLIAN'S EYES FLUTTERED OPEN. SHE LOOKED AROUND, disoriented. No longer on the bench, she curled into the soft blanket wrapped around her body. Her head lay in Ian's lap, his fingers running through her hair.

"Are you beautiful?" His voice was hoarse and tense.

"In this moment I feel beautiful."

His fist tightened in her hair and she moaned.

"You push me to edges, Jillian. I don't know why you challenge me at every turn."

Fear and excitement mixed in her eyes when she looked up at him.

"What do I make you want to do to me?"

His eyes narrowed. A dark and ominous look masked his face.

"Hurt you. Control you. Make you suffer. And bring you pleasure."

Her throat was dry. She ran her tongue over the back of her teeth. A sarcastic remark eluded her addled mind.

"Yes, please."

He reached down and tipped her chin up.

"Please what?" He brushed his lips across hers. "Use your words. Tell me what you want."

Jillian tried to lift her head to kiss, but he pulled back until they barely touched.

"Answer me," he growled.

She let her gaze wander, embarrassed by her desires.

"I want everything you said. All of it. I want to feel your control..." She couldn't finish. The thought of pain and suffering scared her, but right now she felt like she'd try anything for him.

"Are you sure you don't want someone who you can easily control and have great sex?"

It used to be exactly what she wanted, but something in her was always unfulfilled. Right here, right now everything felt possible. She wanted soft, but she also wanted hot, rough and demanding. How could she justify these things to herself after all she'd been through?

"No," she replied. "I need this..."

His low chuckle sounded evil to her ears. "You want me to chain you up and hide you away as my sex slave?"

Jillian frowned and rolled her eyes. "Stop being difficult. You want words."

"Mind them, then. They could get you into trouble."

"Maybe I like trouble."

"I think you are trouble."

"You have no idea." Jillian grinned up at him.

"Oh, I'm getting one. I think the next time I'll turn you over my knee. Then we'll see what words come out of that lovely mouth."

She sat up with a start and stared at him, shaking her head.

"You enjoyed it more than you let on earlier."

Embarrassment flooded her face as she remembered the warm feeling that had spread across her ass earlier.

"I bet you are wet just thinking about it happening."

Jillian shook her head in denial. His hand snaked down her body between her legs. "You're right: you aren't wet, you are soaked."

Unable to stop her body from its need, she spread her legs wider to allow him better access. He plunged two fingers inside, and she leaned back against his hard body.

"Please..." she whispered. "Please..."

His thumb worked across her clit as he added another finger.

"Please what?"

"Please... Oh please... fuck me," she babbled, her body racing once again toward another orgasm.

"Someone is insatiable and demanding."

"I'll do anything you want."

"A dangerous offer, my dear." Her body clenched around his fingers at the words.

Jillian's entire body quivered, the orgasm just out of reach.

"Please... please... fuck me. Let me come, damn it!"

His fingers stopped their movement and pulled out. He brought them to her mouth. "Open."

His fingers pressed against her lip. "Clean up your mess."

She did as he commanded and sucked her juices off his fingers. Jillian felt wound so tight again, her body shook against his. "I need to come."

"No. You want to come. You don't need to come after the amount of orgasms you survived earlier."

"Please," she whined, letting her own hand move between her legs.

He grabbed her wrist and smacked her pussy hard with his other hand. For a moment she moaned and writhed in the wave of pain and pleasure.

"You will not touch yourself without my permission."

"You don't own me."

"No. But you want to explore this again. Don't you?"

Jillian nodded, then remembered herself. "Yes, Ian."

"Good, then this is how we will proceed. Now let's get you dressed and get you home."

CHAPTER TWELVE

"Kade." His voice echoed into the phone.

"Good morning to you too. Everything okay?"

"As much as it can be within the current situation. Is this a business call or a social one?"

"Both," Ian stated with a hard bluntness. "Which would you like first?"

"Let's get business out of the way, and I hope it's excellent news, because I could use some right now."

"My team thinks they've traced Atlas to somewhere near the Boston area. Does that make sense to you?"

On the other end of the phone, Kade let out a lengthy sigh. "That matches up with what Samantha thought she'd just found. It makes perfect sense."

"How so?" Ian pushed.

"It's sort of like being home. Our first dominant lives there."

"You both served the same dominant?" He wasn't sure if he should push the subject, but more information was always better.

"Yes. He was very strict, a disciplinarian in every way. It was his decision that Atlas become a female dominant. He matched us up so we could learn together."

"Why?"

"Because we fit well together. She was smart, liked control, and had her shit together. He knew she'd do well in the trade." Kade sighed.

"Why do I feel a but coming?"

"She never fully settled into the headspace. It was like she put on an armor to please the world and satisfy the directive, but it never seemed to give her what she needed. Don't get me wrong -- you couldn't tell it by watching her. In scene she's magnificent. Every move executed to perfection, every look nailed and to hear her commands. I swear any man or woman would melt at them. Her entire focus was pleasing Dominick in every way, and so she followed his lead until something happened between them. Then she moved to DC. By then she'd perfected the craft as professional dominant which gave her more options. Ultimately, I think it was the pressure of not openly being herself that broke her. When everything else blew up in her perfectly crafted world blew apart, she didn't know how to handle it."

"Makes sense." An interminable pause held the silence between them. "We'll find her, Kade."

"I hope so."

"Reece just needs to get his head out of his ass and pull her back in line. To give him that opportunity, we need to find her."

"Are you sure you are over her?" Ian asked, hoping his friend wouldn't take offense.

"You are never over someone like her. There's a quality in a women like that which sticks with you. Strong, independent, fierce outside and yet if you get on the inside, there's a loyalty and fiery passion that runs even deeper. But I can't give her what she needs, and she can't give me what I need."

"I know the type."

"Speaking of type, how did things go with Jillian? I saw she booked a private room with the cameras off."

"You know you just violated half a dozen club policies with that statement," Ian teased.

"Yep, but the cat's away and all. Besides, I can't remember the last time you used the club's facilities. There's something about this girl, I can tell."

"We played, but I didn't fuck her, if that's what you want to know."

"Well, this is quite the turn of events, Mister I Just Want a Casual Affair. I thought she wasn't your type."

"She's not. This is just an experimental journey for her."

Silence invaded the line.

"I think that's fair," Ian tried to continue.

"You must want this one bad." Kade chuckled.

"Possibly."

"Possibly? So tell me, did you let her just waltz out of the room without any standing orders?"

"I edged her and told her she couldn't come without permission."

"Oh, you've got it really bad."

"Fuck off." There was no point in denying Kade's implication. He barely knew Jillian and had more anxiety over her than he had any right to feel. Going into their agreement, he knew it was only for her exploration, but after their scene he had an almost schoolboy-like crush on her.

"If you want to elaborate on what you did with her, I might be able to tell you why she's running scared."

"Who said she's running scared?"

"It's pretty obvious by the tone in your voice. You are scared you were too intense, or maybe not intense enough, or some other version in between. She hasn't returned your texts in two days and you're scared she won't."

Ian crinkled his brow at the more than accurate assessment from his friend.

"Stop acting so desperate. She's had a tough go of it, according to Samantha. Just let her come to you." Kade sounded smug on the other end of the line and he wanted nothing more than to wipe the look off his friends face.

"I know," Ian retorted.

"No. I don't think you do. When is the last time a woman didn't tell you she was yours just because you looked her way? When did you want a woman who was deeper than just a fall to her knees and suck your cock type?"

Ian shifted in his seat. He'd replayed their time together over and over in his mind. The way she moved, the way her body responded to his. Everything about her reaction screamed how amazing she would be as a slave, but she didn't want a relationship with him. She just wanted to test the waters to get over whatever was in her head.

"Has Samantha said anything?"

"No." Kade sighed. "She's tight-lipped on this one. Usually I can get her to open up a bit, but I think other things have her right on the edge. It sounds like you two have a connection, though."

"There was a spark, and her response in a dynamic is breathtaking."

"Either the scene freaked her out, or she thought about it later and freaked herself out."

"I don't know, man. All I know is she's not talking to me about it, and if that taste of it freaked her out, then it creates a legitimate reason for me to keep my distance and find her someone less intense."

Ian sat and wondered which would be worse for him: if she showed up on Friday night as they'd agreed, or if she cancelled or didn't even show up at all. Maybe he was just imagining the chemistry. The dominant feeling when he'd commanded her in positions or the need he'd held back when he'd pushed her over the edge until she'd cried. Maybe he was just lonely and overly stressed about the multiple projects at work. He barely knew her, he reasoned, and becoming hung up on her so quickly just wasn't logical.

"You're hopeless, you know," Kade said.

"Probably. I'll let you know as soon as the team locates Atlas."

"Thanks."

He hung up the phone and looked down to check the text message for what felt like the hundredth time today. "I need to get a grip."

CHAPTER THIRTEEN

"How was it?" Samantha practically purred as she flicked pool water up on the deck across Jillian's feet. Her expression was one of a Cheshire Cat who seemed to know more than she was telling but wanted the details, anyway.

Jillian hit the off button on her phone and placed it on the table harder than she meant to.

"You should text him."

"I was just checking on my email."

"Yeah. Okay. Tell me another one, Pinocchio. The look on your face tells me you've got it bad."

"Screw you."

"With pleasure. Maybe it will relieve the tension running through your body." Samantha batted her eyes and grinned.

"Fuck off," Jillian retorted, rolling her eyes.

"Well, come over here, beautiful, and I'll do just that."

"You're impossible, you know." Jillian sighed at the fact the deflection had done little to make Samantha change the subject or the fact there was no reason to deny she had it bad for this man. She barely knew him. Their first session had stirred more things inside her then she wanted to admit. Now she swirled with an internal war of guarded independence and the sudden desire to let someone into her world. After just one session she felt almost obsessed. Each movement pushed against another wall. One position flowed into another like the movements of a kata.

After just one session, the intensity of his draw was worse than her first teenage crush. When she'd agreed to the arrangement, she knew it would be intense, but she hadn't expected the number of ways he seemed to make her entire world focus on him. It was just an idiotic crush. She had to get her head on straight. This was not the time to lose her heart or her head to someone who wanted something she couldn't offer.

Jillian stepped up to the side of the pool and dove gracefully into the water with the smallest splash. A couple of laps through the pool would help her burn off the nervous energy and insistent arousal between her legs. Why the hell had he taken her to the edge and not let her come again? Did he think she'd disobey? Everything about it had pushed her right up to the edge of her own dark desires. Here were the fantasies she pushed away to be successful in the world.

When she was done, she leaned against the side of the pool.

"If you'd tell me what Ian did with you, then I could help you plan your next move. You will see him again, right?"

"I'm not one to kiss and tell, Samantha. But I've heard nothing from him since that night, other than a good night text. Besides, this is just casual. Nothing serious. There's no reason to go all gaga over a man who's just being 'nice.' Scraping off the rust until he can pass me off to someone else. Besides, I'm not the slave type."

"Sweetheart, I don't think you remember how to do anything but run away." She bumped her hip against Jillian's.

The words hit Jillian like a slap. Her body recoiled, and she stared at Samantha. "I'm not running away."

"Aren't you? From all appearances things went well the other night and yet here you sit trying to find all the reasons it won't work before it even gets started."

"He wants a slave, Samantha. Do I look like the slave type?"

"Yes." Samantha's words contained no sense of humor. "You look exactly like a woman who wants to drop the mantle of life at the door and let someone make the decisions. A woman who wants to feel cherished, protected, and able to explore your darkest fantasies and desires without reservation."

"That's not me. I've worked too hard to get where I am in life. There's no reason I would just give over all the power I've earned."

"Who said give? Power is earned. Leadership is done by example, not force. What makes you afraid?"

"Losing myself." Jillian flipped the answer back quickly.

"Bullshit. You are more self-aware than most people I know. Stop running. Face the darkness and stop making me be the heavy in these conversations. That's usually your job." Samantha exaggerated a sigh and smiled down at Jillian.

Silence stretched between them, each lost in their own thoughts.

"Ladies." The server startled Jillian. "Kade sent these drinks over for you."

"Tell him we appreciate it, but it won't get him out of him trying to avoid me." Samantha lifted the drink, looked over to the bar, and saluted Kade before he turned, walking away from the area.

"This is unexpected," Jillian quipped to lighten the conversation and mood.

"Yeah. This is his way of telling me he will not tell me things." Samantha grimaced. "On the other hand, maybe it will loosen you enough to enjoy yourself-you tight-ass prude."

Jillian feigned insult. "Tight-ass prude?"

"Yes. Tight-ass prude. Maybe I should make you a T-shirt to warn all the guys before they approach you." Samantha laughed.

"So not true."

"Of course it is-'cause you're too chicken to jump on that crush of yours."

"Really? You are stooping to high school tactics? Don't you think you're a bit old for such things?"

"Nope. It's the only way to get a tight-ass prude to open up. Well, butt plugs and speculums can do it too, but insults seemed easier."

A rushing flush ran across Jillian's face at the casual mention of such intimate items in public.

"Oh come off it. You aren't blushing, are you? There are multiple play spaces and public rooms all over this club."

"I know. It's just... easier to talk about with clients. It's clinical and objective, but when you say it you make it seem so... dark."

"Hon, that's not me. That's your mind pushing against those deep dark desires you keep pushed down inside. I think it's time to open the door and see what's behind it."

CHAPTER FOURTEEN

Jillian flipped the phone in her hand, glad for the quiet day at work. Thoughts of her time with Ian, the feeling of her body as it moved under his command pushed against the entire concept of consensual slavery. It didn't matter if it was just a term; it was primitive to feel a desire to own another person. The idea pushed all of her buttons, not to mention the all-consuming fire between her legs. She couldn't remember the last time she'd felt constantly aroused. All of it pointed to the need to decide or go insane.

Her cell phone danced across her desk, showing the incoming text. She was lost so deep in thought the sound startled her. With a deep breath, she tried to center herself as she picked up the phone.

Meet me at the club at 7pm tonight.

Ian's text caused her body to tense in anticipation, but her brain wasn't over the internal battle.

Presumptuous -- believing I have nothing else to do tonight
but kneel, naked and needy, at your beck and call.

Her fingers rushed over the keyboard. Without a second thought, she hit send. As she read the message, she let out a groan.

Look who's being presumptuous. But I like the image you present and I could get used to you being at my beck and call.

Jillian's fingers shook. Had she misinterpreted his intent? Did he invite her to the club to tell her he wasn't interested?

I'm sorry. I don't know what I was thinking.

The message was pathetic, and she admonished herself for sounding desperate in a medium which contained no tone, although she admitted the fact she'd followed his order about not orgasming was affecting her emotions.

We can discuss it tonight. I'll see you at 7pm. Your name is on the guest list.

For a long moment Jillian stared at the phone. Her thoughts ran wild, and she admonished herself. With an effort, she looked down at the folders on her desk. Jillian picked the folder to her afternoon appointment and reviewed the notes.

As a kink-aware counselor, she saw people from all walks of life. There were just times when Jillian felt like she was drowning in it with no relief. The words she was about to use for a couple who identified as a dominant and submissive in need of sexual counseling swirled in her mind. The last several sessions focused on the concepts of protection, trust, admiration, and respect as the foundation for the exchange of power in their relationship. In session, the concepts were simple to give to others, but she wasn't sure if she was ready to do the same. Yet everything about their first session together felt so right.

A knock at the door caused her head to raise. "Your three o'clock is here."

Jillian smiled at her assistant. "Thanks. Can you send them in please?"

CHAPTER FIFTEEN

The heavy traffic caused Jillian to arrive late at the club. She refused to text and drive, which meant she had not let Ian know of her predicament. By the time she reached the front door, the sexual need combined with the stress of the commute left her frazzled.

Jillian reached the top of the steps just as Ian opened the club's front door. He smiled down at her. Between her legs, her traitorous body demanded attention.

"Hello beautiful." His voice was a deep velvet rumble. "I thought maybe you changed your mind."

"Traffic. Long day," she said. A heavy sigh lifted her body, and she forced a smile.

Ian nodded. "DC traffic is horrible during rush hour. It usually isn't as bad this late. Let's get you inside."

Jillian stepped forward, covering the couple of steps between them with a slight hesitation. On an inhale she caught his scent, short-circuiting her brain.

They walked through the club making small talk about the day.

In the corner of the dining room, a reserved sign sat on a small table, and Ian led them to it.

"I made the presumption you'd be hungry, so I made reservations for dinner." While his words teased, there was steel in his tone. "If you were mine, I wouldn't need to worry if it were a presumption."

For a long moment he stared at her, the lust in his eyes reflecting everything her body felt. With a blink he looked away. The chair scraped across the floor as he pulled it from the table.

With a slight smile, Jillian took the offered seat and placed the cloth napkin across her lap. Ian turned and moved to sit across from her.

"Breathe, Jillian. You look like a naive virgin being led to sacrifice."

The image broke the tension, and she laughed. "I no longer qualify as virginal."

"Did you follow my order since we last saw each other?"

Jillian nodded and pushed her legs together in need.

"Good girl."

The small praise made her smile. What would it be like to be his good girl? And why did such a thought excite her? What they wanted was incompatible. This was just a bit of fun in the meantime.

On the table her fingers wrapped around the wine glass, and Ian reached out to lay his hand on top. The contact raised goose bumps across her body. With a slight hesitation, she forced her eyes to meet his. The intensity was almost palpable. It drew her in and ignited the slow burn he'd set in motion days prior.

They barely noticed as the waiter placed a salad in front of each of them and retreated.

"Did you enjoy me taking control of your pleasure? Refusing to let you come for the last few days?"

She tried to think, but all she could focus on was the increasing throb of her clit. His words stoked her need.

"Yes."

They stared at each other for a long moment. Neither wanted to break the spell which held them in an intense bubble. His gazed ran along her body. Under her shirt, Jillian felt her nipples harden.

"You're turned on," he said.

"Days of denial will do that to a girl."

Ian smiled. "You will always be a challenge, I can see."

"If you can't lift my world, then we're incompatible in a power exchange. Somehow, I think you'll rise to the challenge though."

"Just the right balance of strength and submission. There's no hotter combination."

Jillian pulled her hands back toward her and into her lap. The move evaporated the moment.

"Why are you so guarded, Jillian? You aren't a shy newbie, and your professional experience means this subject isn't taboo."

"What do you mean my 'professional experience'? What are you implying?" Jillian was used to being misjudged for being a sex counselor.

"All I meant was the fact you often discuss various sexual issues and situations with your clients. It's a little surprising to find you so guarded in your own desires."

"We best teach what we must learn." She forced a smile and looked up. "Theory, discussions, and practicum are all very different."

"True."

Silence hung between them. In it, both ate in the stilted tension.

"Why a slave?" Jillian broke the silence, placing her fork across her plate.

"Excuse me?"

"You told me you were looking for a slave. Why?"

"So I'm allowed to lift her world completely."

The answer caught Jillian so off-guard her hand slipped from the wine glass. Most of the time the question garnered an answer about ownership, power or control. Other times it was about the need to dominate everything about another person's world.

"What's in it for you?" She forced the question out on an exhale.

"A partner who gives me what I need to lift. There's nothing more amazing than the trust and adoration of another person. In the exchange of power, it can create a euphoric state for all involved. As a master, I enjoy knowing the relationship is always 'on'. For me, it is a way of life -- a way of being and interacting. The development of the bond which will grow over time for both people. A relationship where my heart and trust are placed in my partner's hands for safekeeping, as much as they place theirs in mine."

The words kicked off a torrent of emotions. It was everything she wanted, but the words, the phrasing were not things she could stand to hear.

"But why do you want a slave?"

"Would the word pet be better?" Ian smiled. "Or an honored object, an inequitable partner in an equitable power exchange or is it that you prefer submissive? Any word can describe a power exchange which is twenty-four by seven, but flexible enough to bend with the events of the world."

"It depends on how the words are used."

Ian nodded.

"Exactly. Each one of those words out of context can cause a problem. For me, the word slave signifies a type of commitment and takes away the meek and mild connotations of the word submissive."

"How so? Most people see a slave in its historic sense, regardless of how it is used in these surroundings. There's nothing more meek and mild than a slave under the whip."

His laugh caught her off-guard. Her face scowled in response.

"None of those words necessarily indicate meekness or mildness. These types of relationship require strength, commitment, and trust."

The words were an intoxicating mix of excitement and fear as they warred with her inner feminist ideals. An odd combination of desire and belonging tinged with just enough intrigue to keep it interesting. In the end, they were just words. Jillian knew from unfortunate experiences the words were often easy to provide, but the action could quickly contradict them.

"How could a slave possibly have power in the relationship?

Doesn't the master have final say in everything? With no voice to be heard, desires to be expressed, how could it be anything but one-sided? This is frustrating. I sound like I'm clueless when I'm not."

Ian smiled.

"You're not clueless. Most people in the scene only glimpse certain parts. They hear one person's point of view and believe it to be the only way. If it goes against their own views or beliefs, an entire part is dismissed. Same with the words. They might have concepts and guidelines, but no two people, let alone groups, define things in the exact same way. I seek a slave because I want someone strong, who speaks their mind within a very structured relationship. For me, it provides much more intense moments."

"It only happens in fantasies and novels. Actual life makes it impossible," Jillian replied, a disappointed sigh slipping through her lips.

"Are you sure?"

The statement was simple. A flare of excitement and hope raced through her.

"Experience tells me I'm right."

"Then you've just not had the right experiences. What did our time together tell you the other night?"

A blush lit across Jillian's face. Her body responded as if his hand, rather than his words, raked along her skin.

"I want to explore this, Jillian. The image of you on your knees has left me in the same state you're currently feeling. You know the one where the tendrils of excitement keep you aroused and waiting -- to give the command in my case and to hear it, in yours. A place where you can letting your world go for just a minute and all your cares, wants, needs, and desires are mine to give or deny."

CHAPTER SIXTEEN

Ian watched her body. The internal struggles ebbed and flowed across her beautiful face in a tapestry of distortions and relief. Each emotion and word was weighed before she moved to the next one. The result was exquisite.

"Ownership is such an ugly word." Her voice came out rushed.

"There's freedom in the relief of certain burdens in life. To live life rather than simply surviving it in a vain attempt to prove worth. A submissive continuously weighs and balances their submission with each action. There is a need for self first, then a bow to their dominant partner. A slave already knows their partner's focus is on them and in return is freed to offer the same. Maybe it is a bit of a romantic notion, but all the same, it is what I see is possible in you."

Ian watched her breath quicken when she placed her hand over her heart. Her gaze fell to the table in front of him.

"Put that way, it sounds beautiful." The words tumbled forth in a whisper.

"Do you trust me enough to see what it is like in reality?"

Jillian nodded.

"Words, Jillian. This is too important to simply let the smallest movement signify your consent or denial of decision. We either move forward together or we don't move forward at all."

"I'm scared."

"I know." Ian placed his open palm up on the table. "It takes two to succeed or fail. Thus, neither can be left behind. Shall we walk this together for a bit and see if it suits us?"

He watched the hesitation fight with the desire to jump. In this moment, everything he'd ever worked to achieve, every desire he'd asked to obtain, sat across from him. To master a woman this amazing was more than he'd ever hoped.

"I trust you, Sir." The calm words were punctuated with a penetrating look which ran straight through his heart and down to his groin.

Ian smiled. "Then kneel beside me without saying another word."

He watched her body tense. Each muscle bunched and released in time with the storm of emotions across her face. She moved her hand to her lap without moving her gaze.

With deliberate movement, she stood. Jillian's chin jutted upward, her gaze moving away from Ian. Each calculated step moved her around the table until she stood beside his chair. She filled her lungs with a deep inhale, and he watched her gracefully fold her frame until she knelt beside him.

Around the room it was as if a collective breath exhaled when Jillian settled beside him. He could hear murmurs of "beautiful," "exquisite," "graceful," and "lucky." Internally, he agreed with each one of them.

"Thank you for the beautiful gift." He leaned down and whispered into her ear. "See how thrilling a few simple words can make the evening change course."

Ian picked up his water glass in a casual attempt to settle his own excitement. For a long moment, he enjoyed the furtive gazes tossed his way. Beside him, Jillian knelt in perfect stillness, but her excitement grew more evident.

"Let's go put you out of your misery--or is it causing you more delicious misery?" Ian said and looked down to the kneeling form beside him to watch as her head snapped around to meet his gaze.

Ian stood and offered his hand to help her stand. With little effort, Jillian unfolded until she once again stood beside him. "See, it's as easy as riding a bike in the right circumstances."

Jillian smiled and nodded.

"It seems you've lost your words, my dear, but I must say this blush is beautiful."

CHAPTER SEVENTEEN

A thousand thoughts ran through Jillian's head as they passed through the hallways of the club. Ian had placed her hand in the crook of his arm when he'd helped her from the kneeling position beside him. When he'd said the words which had propelled her to her knees beside him, a state of uncontrolled panic and excitement ran through her with an intensity she'd never experienced. Everything about it made her feel safe and openly vulnerable in the same instance. The excitement which coursed through her felt like walking through a mental cloud.

Ian's voice pulled her out of her own head. "Jillian."

"Yes, Sir?" she responded.

"There you are. I thought maybe I'd lost you in your mental wonderland."

"I'm sorry. It's just..."

"No reason to apologize. It will be okay." His voice stopped. She looked up and met his patient gaze and smile. "Much better."

"Thank you, Sir," Jillian whispered.

"When I open this door, I want you to walk over to the large chair on the right. Kneel in front."

Jillian nodded. She felt her unsteady breath increase its pace as the panic outweighed the excitement.

"There's nothing to fear here, Jillian," Ian said. His voice was calm and steady. There was no hint of disapproval or judgement. "You lose nothing by walking this path. It takes a strong woman to make the choice to kneel to another. One who knows herself and trusts this knowledge. None of those things change."

For a minute she mentally leaned on his calm voice. Each word added support and fought off the darkness which threatened to consume her.

"That's it. Deep breaths. This is a path we walk together, inequitably in some way and very equitable in others, but always together. We step when we are both ready to step, we hold when either of us needs to hold. This will always be true."

She inhaled deeply. The light smell of his cologne surrounded her, but other than her hand on his arm, they weren't touching, yet the sparks of electricity in this simple connection ran through her.

In front of her, the door loomed and called in the same instant. She longed to see if his words were true while battling against the repulsion of the words he used. There was no denying the rising excitement of each moment leading up to this one. She waited on her knees in front of him for his next words and commands to push them both over the precipice of daring and excitement.

No matter the internal arguments or reason, her body responded in rapid anticipation. It fed a hunger she'd denied for far too long, and right before her was the offer of a feast. Jillian inhaled deeply. Thoughts and needs raced through her mind unbidden. Here was a safe opportunity for her to finally move forward into this world and bravely face herself again--or know for certain these needs would never be satisfied.

It took everything in her to push away the past, to set down the baggage at the door and accept that Ian was different. To believe the words would become actions and he'd not strip away her dignity, strength or needs to make her forcefully subservient without merit.

She needed to move forward. To push through all the past and fearlessly grab what she wanted with both hands. Here she was safe. In this space there would be no abuse, no lowering of self to make her partner feel bigger, no need to step into weakness to make Ian feel stronger. The words felt right. Different somehow than before, but until actions verified them, they could still ring hollow.

The slow deep breaths did nothing for the tight knot of nerves balled in her stomach.

"Just jump."

Jillian startled at the unexpected words, and with an effort, placed both hands on the door and pushed it open as the last vestiges of fear as she stepped into this brave unfamiliar world.

CHAPTER EIGHTEEN

Jillian's body tensed and relaxed. Her internal struggle was etched across her face, but he knew she'd take the next step. He needed her to take a leap of faith and trust him. It didn't matter what they called the relationship or what it looked like; he craved Jillian like a dying man in the desert craved water.

Her body sauntered across the room. The swing of her tight ass made his cock twitch in his pants and he bit back a moan as he followed behind her. With grace, her body folded into a kneeling position next to the chair. Ian admired her body for a long minute until he finally sat down in front of her.

"We will start at our own foundation." The tone of his voice held an authority, though the tone was soft. "Communication is the key to everything. How we understand each other. To signal intent in quiet hand motions from across the room, a set of commands that give a quick understood explanation or a body position which expresses a need words cannot express."

Jillian breath rose and fell in slow shallow intakes then changed to sharp intakes when he spoke. Everything about her body language told him something about her. In this space it was his responsibility to learn her signals just as much as it was her responsibility to learn his.

"Let's start with posture and poses this evening while learning both audio and silent commands. A place to establish our way of moving forward and erase the past mistakes of others." Her shoulders relax.

"The body is both malleable and rigid depending on where the mind carries it. Where is your mind leading your body, Jillian?"

The question startled Jillian out of her obvious internal dialogue.

"I know you are nervous, but to make this work both of us you need to be engaged, and I asked you a question."

"I'm sorry, Ian." She looked down at the hands in her lap.

"For what?"

"Um... not paying attention to the question. My mind is racing and my body is more aroused than I've ever remembered being in my life."

Ian shifted in his seat, and Jillian looked up. His face was stern but not aggressive.

"You live in your head too much."

"A hazard of my job I suppose," she replied.

"Then this is where we start. Stand and strip. From now on, the hand signal for strip is this." His hand made a 'Z' formation in the air. "When you see it, you will stop and remove your clothes. Is that clear?"

"Yes."

His hand made the formation in the air again and he waited.

Jillian hesitated. Emotions flew across her face and she shifted in the kneeling position.

"Were my instructions unclear?" His tone was harder this time.

"No," she nearly whispered.

"Then let's not get off on the wrong foot. Get moving, girl."

He watched the command take hold of her internal conversation, and she nodded.

With the grace of a dancer, she rolled her body back and lifted it across her toes until she stood before him. Practiced hands moved down her blouse and worked to remove it. Each piece of clothing followed until they were in a pile at her feet.

"Neatly place your clothes on the counter to the right of the door. Return and stand in the center of the room facing the mirror. This hand signal means go now and do the task you're assigned."

With his forefinger and middle finger pointing out and the rest of his hand curled in, he pointed towards the shelf.

Jillian squatted, retrieved the pile and folded them with care. Then she lifted them and walked across the room to set them on the designated shelf.

Her focus become more singular as the task went on, moving out of her head and into the moment. When she finally stood in the middle of the room, he could see a new forced calm.

Ian closed his hand in a fist and pointed his forefinger to the floor.

"This signal means come immediately and stand at this spot. Which brings us to our first position. This one is standing rest. Here you will take instruction, wait patiently, or focus on me without looking at me. As I don't prefer the look of a military-style attention, I will use this posture most often." He walked around her while he spoke. Each round made her body became more rigid, less relaxed and focused on him.

"Place your right hand at the small of your back and cup your left hand in it. Your feet should be the width of your shoulders. Shoulder blades down. Head level and eyes facing forward without moving from a focused spot. It does not matter if I touch you, or you are replying to a question, your head should not move."

He watched her hands move to her back and her feet spread a slight distance. Her head was raised slightly but still angled down.

Ian worked her body into the form he desired. His hands pressed on her shoulder blades until her shoulders dropped to the corrected position. Then he moved her head until it was level.

"This is how this position should look every time." He raked his hand up her thigh lightly. Her body shivered in anticipation against him. "If my hand were to move higher, what would it find?"

Jillian stared straight ahead, her mouth slightly agape. Days of frustration surged to the surface.

Ian stood upright, swatted her ass with a riding crop he'd picked up while she'd put her clothes away, and growled quietly in her ear, "I asked you a question."

"You'd find me... excited."

"The first time I ask the questions, you answer it. Even if it is to ask for more time to form a full answer."

"Yes, Ian."

His hand brushed at the apex of her legs. Jillian's shuttered breath made him smile.

One again, his hand closed in a fist. This time the first two fingers pointed to the ground.

"This signal is to kneel, legs closed at this point."

Without another word, he lifted his hand and gave the signal again.

Jillian fell to her knees in front of him, her back straight and eyes forward. Again, Ian adjusted her posture lightly. Her previous training was evident.

"Next, is the command for kneel-open." He smiled at their image in the mirror.

He placed his hand in the position for kneel, then spread his two fingers apart.

At the command, Jillian adjusted her position until her knees were almost shoulder width apart.

He saw her watching him in the mirror and finally squatted down behind her.

"This is one of my favorite positions. It is both strong and vulnerable." His hand ran up her back. "In it one can easily read the state of a person. If they are distracted, their head falls forward, while someone who is tired may slump. Then there is a person who is fully focused and attentive. Each brush against the skin can set a body on the edge. I imagine after days of following my instructions, anticipating what this evening might bring, you are quite focused and alerted to your own state of arousal."

Jillian's breath caught.

CHAPTER NINETEEN

The electric thrum coursing through her body caught Jillian's attention. She could feel the arousal between her legs intensify under his gaze. In this moment, the world went quiet. It was unusual and welcomed in her recently chaotic life.

Behind her, she watched him stand and walk across the room, back to the chair which looked like a throne. When he sat, he held her gaze. Without another word, his hand formed into a fist and two fingers pointed down, then parted.

A thrill of excitement rushed through her. Jillian pulled her legs together and rolled back across her toes until she stood in the middle of the floor. With purposeful strides, she walked toward Ian, then once again descended in a kneeling position and splayed her legs open to his view.

"Beautiful," Ian murmured.

The small word settled the final bit of nerves and she relaxed into the position.

"There are two more silent commands I want to teach you tonight," he said, as his fist rolled parallel to the floor. Two fingers went out and curled back in, then repeated the motion.

"This is the command to masturbate," he said with an even tone. "When my hand goes flat out and moves back and forth, it is the command to immediately stop."

His hand mimicked the words.

Once again his fingers curled toward him. Jillian inhaled and let her hand drift between her thighs. Her fingers met with the slickness of her growing arousal.

"Look at me. You can see any silent commands I give you from your periphery."

She looked up into his eyes. The hunger and intensity surprised her. It also fed the deep need to be wanted and desired.

With focus, she let her hand work through her wet folds. So many recent nights were spent touching herself like this, imagining him commanding her to show him the efforts of his standing order.

Jillian let a finger skim across the edge of her clit and her eyes closed as a groan pushed past her lips.

"Look at me. If you can't look at me, then maybe I need to do the task myself."

Her eyes shot open. She'd already experienced his expert ability to extract pleasure and pain from her body, making the choice to obey or disobey an easy one.

"That's it. Pleasure yourself like it is my hand between your thighs." Ian spoke in a hoarse command.

Jillian let her hips move with the rhythm of her hand. Each stroke stoked the banked fire Ian produced with his standing command from their last encounter.

In short order, her body gave over to the built-up need and she moaned in pleasure. Her fingers moved faster through her slit and up, around her clit and back down. Each rotation pushed her closer to orgasm until she sat right on the edge.

She let her head move to keep eye contact with Ian, but the impending orgasm pressed against her ability to focus.

Just as the orgasm built to its edge, Ian moved his flat hand back and forth. Everything in Jillian wanted to scream, but her fingers lay still on the side of her thigh.

"Very nice," Ian purred. "You need to learn, on this path, your body is mine. Every orgasm is one I grant. Control and structure are a way of being."

The words settled against Jillian's inner core and took root.

CHAPTER TWENTY

Ian's hand once again curled two fingers in a command to masturbate. Jillian's fingers worked softly around her clit. Out of the corner of her eyes, she saw him pull something from his pocket. He leaned forward, fingers pinching the tip of each nipple, tugging and pulling until they were hard pebbles. His action pushed her against the edge again. Right before the wave took her, he motioned the command to stop.

In his hands, a pair of silver clips, connected with a silver chain, moved toward her taut nipples. Pain rushed through the sensitive buds and shoots straight down her body, mixing with the pleasure in an euphorically erotic way. A moan escaped her as the second clip latched on.

"Looks like not all pain is scary," Ian mused and gave the command to continue masturbating.

His fingers scraped across the back of the clips and a bite of pain rushed through Jillian's body.

"Please. I can't hold on," Jillian begged.

"If you come before I grant it, I will punish you," Ian stated. "I want you exposed. To let your guard down. From here, I want you to know your pleasure comes from me. You will come, or not, when I command it."

"Please," she whispered.

Jillian's fingers did not slow as she absorbed his words. Her eyes were fixed on his, but always waiting for the command to stop.

"Come for me," Ian commanded.

Jillian screamed in relief as the orgasm crashed across her. With each spasm, her body bucked against her fingers. Just when she didn't think she could take any more, Ian pulled the clamps from her nipples. The rush of blood sent her body into another crashing wave. Pain and pleasure mixed through her body, contracting and releasing in a bid to meet days of pent-up need.

Her body fell forward in spent relief until she finally spiraled back down to earth. When she lifted her head to meet his gaze, her eyes were glassy and marked with a look of satisfaction.

Ian sat back in his chair.

"Lick your fingers clean."

Jillian hesitated, but brought them up to her lips. Her scent lingered in the room as her fingers, covered in her juices, hovered right before her lips. Delicately, she licked them thoroughly until Ian nodded in satisfaction.

She waited, quietly, for his next command.

For a long minute, he watched her. The change was apparent. Here in this space, the world melted away and he could see the possibilities that didn't seem likely before.

Jillian knelt in the quiet, letting it surround her. It wasn't the first time this scene had played out in her life, but each time held the unique possibility of a new road and relationship that might "stick." For now, all she wanted to do was revel in the release he'd given her body after demanding it stay on the edge for days.

Ian patted his leg.

"Head here." The command was soft and caring.

She crawled over until she was beside him and lay her head in his lap.

His fingers tangled in her hair, then released and stroked through it.

"Now that we've relieved the initial tension and anticipation..." Ian started.

Jillian smiled.

"I thought it would be prudent to give you a place to start. Alternative names for positions along with new signals to get you there. It seems it's been some time since you've stepped into this place and let yourself go." His voice was steady and calm, which belied the bulge in his pants.

"It looks like you have needs that I can take care for you." She spoke in a murmur.

Ian smiled down at her.

"A dominant who can't control their own needs doesn't have enough control to handle others. If I want a person to do more than just give me themselves periodically, to surrender to me, then I need to be in control of self. Even when the body makes my needs obvious."

"I can help."

"You can follow orders," he admonished softly. "In this place, your entire world is now mine. When we walk through those doors, your focus is on the next command I might give. It does not matter if it is verbal or silent, nor what the command tells you to do. Outside these doors, we are equals-for now."

"How do I know the rules?"

"Just like earlier, I will give them over time. Sometimes formally, others will be practical lessons, until you can almost anticipate the next command and need. Like a dance. When I step, you step to follow."

"It sounds beautiful when you put it into flowery words," Jillian said lazily.

"In here is my domain. It may expand or it may dissolve, but it will not be questioned." He let his words sink in. "Now you've had a taste-do you still wish to proceed?"

Silence lingered in the room. Their collective breaths bounced against the wall. Ian didn't move, but Jillian felt his muscles tense beneath her hand.

"Yes, Ian. I want to proceed. Everything in me tells me to be cautious, but I'm tired of not going for it out of fear. Those times never served me well. I've always held back, but those situations ended in the same pain I tried to prevent." Jillian's voice trembled slightly, but she spoke with confidence.

Above her, Ian smiled.

"In this room I am yours. Outside this place, I am my own, even when we play like we did with a standing command. I've worked too hard to hand over my world to someone I'm getting to know-no matter how amazing I find him."

"Understood," Ian stated. "I'm glad we've established your boundaries and more than glad you enjoyed my standing commands over a few days which brought you more pleasure."

The grin across Ian's face made her laugh. He looked like a mischievous boy with a new toy.

"In that same vein, I would like to try something. I've bought you a present. Please go retrieve it from the shelf by the door and grab your phone." He nodded his head in the direction as he spoke.

Jillian rose with grace and stepped toward the door. On the shelf was a medium-sized wrapped box. Trepidation filled her, but she pushed through the feeling and moved back toward Ian.

As she approached, Ian silently signaled her to kneel. In front of him, she fell to her knees.

"Open it."

With shaky hands, Jillian unwrapped the box. On the front, a bright pink egg with a strange-looking tail was pictured.

"It's a teledildonic toy," Ian explained.

"A what?" Jillian looked up in genuine confusion.

"It's a remote toy I can control via internet and your phone." Ian grinned. "Based on your schedule, I thought our work days might be more interesting."

"Wait. You want me to use this toy while I'm at work?"

"Only on days when you aren't seeing clients. Think of it as a way to encourage you to focus on more things in life."

"It could be interesting." Jillian tried to remain non committal, but just the thought of the entire concept excited her. Everything in her wanted to say yes, but how do you give up that kind of control?

Ian studied her face. The emotions played across it like a movie.

"Just jump, Jillian. You ultimately keep the control. If you want it to stop, you only need to close the application," Ian reassured her. "And when you feel daring, open it and let me take control. Just like here."

With an effort, Jillian nodded.

"Excellent. Let's take it for a spin now."

"Now?"

"Yes, Jillian. This way I can enjoy your reaction and you know exactly what to expect."

For the next few minutes, Ian talked Jillian through the setup process. When they finished, he handed her a small pack of lube.

"Now insert it."

Jillian spread her legs and pushed the toy inside. The egg shape sat against her g-spot while the tails end lay against the edge of her clit. Once complete, she looked up at Ian, who gave the silent command for her to spread her legs wide and place her hands on her thighs.

"Beautiful." His voice came out in a hoarse whisper.

In the silence, he let his eyes linger on her face until they met. In that moment, his fingers scroll against the controls. The vibrator lit up and Jillian startled. He smiled when a moan escaped her.

Not taking his eyes off her, he manipulated the controls to

different levels and patterns, noting results of each change. Jillian's breaths came in pants as the patterns pushed her closer to orgasm.

"Please," she panted.

At her utterance, the vibrations died, and she fell forward.

"Oh my God." The words pushed between a prayer and swear.

"Welcome to my world." Ian looked down and caresed her cheek.

CHAPTER TWENTY-ONE

Jillian stared out the window. Her focus wavered. A deep sigh escaped as a pencil bounced off the desk. The sound of her desk phone startled her out of her daydream.

"Good afternoon, Dr. Hart's office," Jillian said into the receiver out of rote habit.

"What the hell's going on, Jillian? I thought you would call me yesterday," an angry male voice growled into the phone.

"My apologies, Dr. Ratcliffe," she punctuated his name and title. "Life got a little busy."

"I worry about you. You said you were unnerved about a client and needed an immediate consult, then didn't follow up. In our line of work that's a tense signal to send out."

"I'm sorry. I needed to shake a recent couple of sessions off and distracted myself."

"That doesn't sound like you. You aren't unnerved by your clientele and you never need to shake it off. Come to think of it, the 'sorry' part is strange too. Tell me what's going on-or do I need to come over and talk about it face to face?"

Jillian sighed. Brad Ratcliffe knew her better than almost any of her friends. They had gone to grad school together, dating through most of it. In the end, Jillian broke it off to focus on her new practice. Eventually they readjusted their relationship and found it suited them much better. Now he was the person she called when life tilted a little and needed another point of view with her clients and even her own life.

"How about you come over? Maybe a little face to face and background will prove I'm just overreacting." She forced a smile on her face and hoped it translated to her voice.

"You don't overreact to anything. I'll be there in fifteen minutes. Let me clear part of my schedule with my office manager, and before you say it, if it wasn't important enough for me to do that, then you wouldn't have called. See you shortly." Without waiting for anything further, the line went dead.

Jillian stood up and paced the office. Maybe she was just overreacting. With so much changing in her personal life, maybe this client just felt more tilted than he was in life.

Less than fifteen minutes later, the knock on the door drew her attention, and she stood to greet Brad.

"You didn't need to clear your schedule for me."

"When you called you knew what would happen, thus I know it's important. Let's sit and discuss what's on your mind."

"Trying to take over my office?" Jillian asked, a smile playing across the corners of her mouth.

"Making sure you focus and don't blow off the gut feeling that made you pick up the phone," Brad said as he ushered her to the seating arrangement in her office. "So tell me about this client of yours."

"He's just... I don't know how to describe it. He's obsessed with a person. I mean, I know he's got a tragic past, but this feels calculating. Good God, you'd think after years of counseling him and going through so many things to keep his life moving it would be easy. He's brilliant, but something just isn't right. And I feel bound by all of these privacy laws." Jillian studied the edge of the couch and braced for Brad's reaction.

"I'm presuming we're discussing the same client who kicked up similar feelings a few years ago."

Jillian nodded her confirmation.

"You know my opinion on him. He's a predator and always will be. I know we're supposed to believe we can *fix* people - although let's be honest, we only help the people that want help and only in the way they want it - but there are people who turn that brilliance into something dark. Speaking in Hypotheticals, what's not sitting right with you? Do you feel like he's a danger to this object of his? I presume he still refers to them that way?"

"You know it is literally our day job to fix people." Jillian watched Brad roll his eyes, but he didn't interrupt. "Hypothetically, his wording changed. It is more obsessive. He's had a violent past too. The worst part is he's got more money than God."

"That's always an exacerbating factor," Brad admitted. "Why do you think this one is different? Is he changing or is it the influence of this unknown person in his life? If you feel like this new person is at risk, you know you are obligated to protect them from a potential danger, even if it ultimately moves the risk from them to you."

Jillian nodded. "Yes. Money is exacerbating the situation, in my professional opinion."

"What else can you share without violating your privacy concerns?" Brad leaned forward and set his elbows on his knees. His eyebrows furrowed. "As a *consulting colleague,* there is some gray area we can dance in here."

"As you know, I've been his therapist for years."

"Right. So talk to me, what is your genuine concern? What aren't you telling me?"

"His language changed. I didn't realize he'd asked her to marry him. He told me he wanted to give her the world. Keep her so that no one else could have her. To be under her boot, so it was only him she controlled. I don't know their actual relationship, so I don't know if he's being literal or metaphorical. It's like a backwards riddle talking with him."

"That sounds strange," Brad acknowledged.

"How can you keep someone in what amounts to a gilded cage and yet believe they are in control?" Jillian threw the question out but pondered it internally. "I don't know. That's the part that is unclear. I know he was seeing a dominatrix at one point, but I can't imagine she would be the object. But his wording is so odd. He's become much more certain about his ability to 'obtain his prize' recently."

"With this obsession, it can easily turn. Do you feel she is a willing participant here? Your description make it feel vaguely ominous. Do you know enough about the woman in question to confirm her safety?"

"No. I've tried. He won't even tell me her name, just that she's beautiful, amazing and perfect for him. When I try to get close to the subject, he shuts down in an almost Gollum-like possession. Telling me she is his."

A long pause lingered in the conversation. Fear rippled down Jillian's spine.

"Do you think she's at risk? Is he a danger to her?" Brad asked, giving her own fear tangible wording.

"That is the worry. But there's nothing I can do. I have no name or even confirmation she's not just a delusion of his mind, but this feels different from his past issues. He's never focused on a person so exclusivity. A business, an idea or a concept-sure. The obsession lasts until it is obtained and then fades away."

"Which is why you called me. You wanted me voice your own concerns." Brad looked up and met Jillian's eyes. "I think you should be concerned about this woman. If she is 'obtained' and left in her gilded cage to rot because he lost interest and found other business, idea, or concept to amuse himself, what would become of her? Or would a person *fade away* in his world? Does an interactive situation drive his obsession deeper and more violent?"

"Or she could be some figment of his imagination or someone he is fixated on and will never act against, but in my professional opinion, the possibility that this is a real woman and what he may do to her to make her *his* - let alone what may happen after she's in the cage - is a risk I fear."

"Looks like your next move is to flush out her name and see if other agencies need to get involved," Brad said and glanced at his watch. "I have an appointment I need to prepare for. I know you owe me nothing here, but I'm genuinely interested in seeing how this turns out. I hope you'll indulge my piqued curiosity after your next session?" Brad smiled and stood.

"I will, to the extent I can. Thanks for listening. I appreciate your perspective. This case keeps me up at night. Next time we talk, I should tell you about this new guy in my life... Ian."

"New guy? Most definitely. I need to hear something positive going in your life. You get so wrapped up in these cases I feel you lose something of yourself in them."

Jillian quirked an eyebrow.

"Really?" she deadpanned.

"Yes. Yes. I know that's the pot calling the kettle black, but do as I say rather than as I do and all that." Brad held up his hand in defense.

Jillian chuckled. "It's true. Ian's a great guy. I'm unsure of the path we're moving down, but I'm happy for now."

"I can't wait to hear about it. Jacqueline will be happy to hear about your new beau, but I'll leave it to you to bring it up. Perhaps we can have you over for dinner sometime soon and you can broach the subject with her? Maybe fondue and plans to invite this Ian character over with you on a future date?" Brad looked hopeful.

"Yes, soon. Have your assistant call mine to throw something on our collective calendars. I can't wait- and dinner sounds lovely."

"Sounds good." Brad smiled and reached out to give her a hug.

She watched him walk out the door. The conversation made her feel both happy about his reaction to her new love interest and very concerned about the situation with her client.

CHAPTER TWENTY-TWO

Ian sat at his desk looking out across the DC skyline. His mind ran full of distractions. Each one settled right back on Jillian. He recalled her smiles. The way she looked on her knees. The pen twirled on his desk by fingers that needed to fidget.

"Jillian, what are you doing to me?" he said out loud to no one.

The knock at the door startled him out of his reverie.

"Kade is here to see you, Sir," Beth, his administrative assistant, said from the door.

"Send him in." Ian glanced up just as Kade crossed the threshold.

"My apologies for interrupting." Kade preempted further greeting. "I have information that's important."

"No need to apologize. How can I help?"

"We've found her." The simple reply bounced off the walls.

"That's marvelous news," Ian started.

"But..." Kade interrupted.

"Why is there always a but?"

"She is safe- for now. I'm flying up to put my eyes on the situation as it stands and work to get more intel."

Ian nodded and made notes in the case file.

"Dominick called me." Kade's voice wavered.

The look on his face told Ian there was more to the situation than he was sharing.

"She's at his house in Boston. According to Dominick, he thinks she's scared for her life. If that's true, we've missed something huge as her security team." Kade's head dropped.

"Or it means your protectee is well versed in invasion techniques and didn't give you a clue about what was happening. Didn't Atlas go through classes in kidnapping, invasion and self-defense when she moved down here?"

Kade nodded.

"Yeah, but I thought it was to use in a scene. To give her an edge. Something extra. I should have realized she'd take the training to heart. I'm sure it's the reason we've worked to find her and, until now, came up empty."

"Smart woman. She controlled all the pieces."

"So it seems."

"The question is, why does Dominick know where she's at?" Ian asked.

"She wanted to come in out of the cold. One day she showed up in his class and fell right back into her *spot*, so to speak. I think she hit a wall and wanted it to end. Samantha thought she'd found a photo of her on social media, but Dominick called while she was confirming."

"What's the next move then, and what do you need from my team to help?"

"I'm flying up to see her. Take a couple beats to assess the situation and go from there. Since I am obviously missing pieces, I don't know the support I'll require."

"Whatever you need, even if it's a jet to get out of the country." Ian tried to lighten the mood a bit. Atlas was safe, and it lifted a vast weight from his friends shoulders.

"Don't even joke. I might call you for exactly that." Kade forced a smile.

"Just need twelve hours notice, man."

"You sound serious." Kade quirked an eyebrow.

Ian just smiled.

"I am hoping it doesn't come down to something that drastic. Maybe this is all just a severe case of burnout and she just ran to get away from the politic blowback of Reece's sister."

"That would be the ideal reason," Ian agreed. "Did you ever follow up on your suspicions about her client?"

"To the best of our ability. There are no complaints at the club. Outside a proposal for marriage and the video tape of a conversation in her office, there are no indications he's attached to anything malicious. Apart from the disappointment of rejection."

"Then all indications are she ran. It doesn't feel right, though."

"I know, man. But we both know the simplest explanation is usually the most likely."

"True," Ian replied.

"I'll let you know when I get wheels down and see her," Kade said. "Now I hear things are going well between you and a certain person at the club."

Ian chuckled at the abrupt change of the topic. He knew from it that something was still bothering Kade, but he wasn't ready to share.

"Yes. Things are going swimmingly, as they say."

"Well, don't fuck it up, man. Samantha will never let me hear the end of it." Kade smiled.

"Oh, I have every intention of fucking- just not fucking it up."

"It's good to see you happy."

Ian smiled. "It's a foreign feeling, but it feels good."

Kade checked his watch. "I need to go grab stuff. I've got wheels up in 12 hours and I need to settle the club before I leave."

"Good luck. Let me know if there's anything you need- no matter the request."

"I will."

"Seriously, Kade." Ian's voice took on an edge.

"I know. That's what scares me about you," Kade replied and headed for the door.

CHAPTER TWENTY-THREE

Jillian stared at the cursor blinking back at her. Everything in her mind raced. She wanted it to all go away for a few minutes, but a daunting amount of paperwork lay before her. The pencil in her hand bounced on the desk. Her mind roamed from the conversation with Brad back to being on her knees in front of Ian.

In front of her was a patient's case file which puzzled her and frightened her a bit. Yet she couldn't keep her mind in the right place to focus on all the pieces and find the part she felt was missing. With a sigh, she stretched the muscles in her neck.

The cell phone on her desk vibrated, and she smiled at the unique pattern, glad for the sudden respite.

Hello, Jillian.

The text lit up across her screen.

Hello, Ian.

Her fingers slid across the screen.

Is your afternoon open?

I need to get paperwork done.

Are you seeing clients?

Not this afternoon.

Is your new toy in your bag?

The question made Jillian pause. The toy was in her bag, but she didn't know if she was brave enough to use it in the office.

Yes.

Let's try that again. Is your new toy in your bag?

Yes, Sir.

Much better. Want to play?

Now??

Excitement and arousal flared through her.

Yes. Now.

Her fingers hesitated for a long moment, right over the screen when it rang. Automatically she clicked to answer.

Why the hesitation?

Ian's text came after she didn't respond for more than two minutes.

I'm in the office.

So am I.

It's not the same and you know it.

Jillian rolled her eyes glad there was no one around to see it.

We can even things out a bit. Video call?

The unexpected request caught her off-guard. Here was a chance to live a little. To jump off the cliff with a safety net.

Okay.

Her reply was timid and uncertain.

In seconds, Ian's smiling face appeared on her phone.

"Hello, beautiful."

Jillian smiled back, but her fingers shook as she put the phone on its holder on top of her desk.

"Go lock your office door." Ian's soft command worked to guide her down the path.

"Yes, Sir." She stood up, walked to the door, and peeked her head out.

"Hey, Sally," she called to her receptionist. "Why don't you take a long lunch."

"Are you sure?" Sally looked up, surprise written all over her face.

"Yeah. We've been busy lately and I'm just going to work on some paperwork."

"If you're sure. It would be nice to get a lunchtime pedicure." Sally said and smiled.

"Take your time, no rush." Jillian smiled as her fingers fidgeted with the doorknob.

Sally grabbed her bag and keys from the bottom drawer of her desk.

"Can I bring you back anything?"

"No thanks. Have fun."

Sally stepped around and gave a light wave. "Thanks!"

Once she disappeared out of the office, Jillian shut the door and locked it. Anticipation and excitement thrummed through her. She'd never dared to do something so scandalous before.

Jillian took a deep breath and walked back to her desk. She pulled the toy out of her bag and set it in front of her as she settled into her chair.

"Nervous?" Ian asked.

"Yes, Sir."

"Must be some door." He smirked.

"I told my receptionist to take a long lunch."

"So you are alone in your office?" His eyebrow quirked.

"Yes, Sir."

"How about I come over for lunch?"

"I thought we would play by video chat." Jillian tried to keep the disappointment out of her voice.

"Oh, we'll do that too." Ian smiled. "If you're up to lunch, text your office address. Then I want to see your mouth lubricate that toy."

Jillian picked up her phone and typed in her address. Once she hit send and resettled the phone, she picked up the toy. With minimal thought, she plunged ahead, brought the toy to her mouth, and licked the tip.

CHAPTER TWENTY-FOUR

"All the way in that lovely mouth of yours, Jillian," Ian encouraged.

Jillian closed her eyes and pushed the pink egg into her mouth. Her lips came back together once it seated itself inside.

Ian groaned his approval. "Now you've lubricated it so nicely, spread your legs, pull your panties aside and push it home."

Her breath stuttered at his words, but she pulled the egg carefully from her mouth and did as he asked. No sooner did she slip it into her wet pussy than it vibrated. Jillian panted through the initial shocks through her system.

"Beautiful," Ian murmured. "Open your eyes and look at me."

For a moment Jillian debated following his command. Her eyes fluttered open, and she saw his video call shake with his movements.

"I'll be there in 15 minutes. Until then, enjoy." Without another word, he clicked off the video.

The toy in her sprang to a new level before dropping into nothingness. Each wave pushed her closer to an orgasm, then brought her back from the edge once more.

Without an audience, she felt silly sitting in office. As soon as the thought took hold, the toy demanded her attention. Repeatedly it wanted more from her. Time passed without thought while the toy demanded her orgasm, only to deny her once again. Thought disappeared.

The knock on the door startled her out of her reverie. Fear snaked through her body.

Jillian, I am at your office door.

Ian's text came across her phone's screen.

Crawl and open the door on your knees.

As soon as she stood, the toy vibrated relentlessly. She looked around her office, the place of her own domain and space. Did she dare do as he asked?

She still questioned the decision as her knees hit the floor. Each move across the floor was an external and internal decision to move forward. With the final movement traversing the last part of the office, she lay a shaky hand on the door handle and took a deep breath.

The toy continued its relentless pursuit. Her hand turned the door handle, and the toy died in place when the door pushed open in front of her.

Jillian fell back on her knees, her face flushed and breath erratic.

"Hello, my dear," Ian said as he stepped into her office, his own frustration straining against the front of his pants.

Ian gave her the silent signal to rise. When she put her body in motion, the vibration almost put her back on her knees. Once she stood in front of him, the movement inside once again died.

"Breathtaking," Ian whispered against her ear. "Everything in me wants to fuck you across your desk, but this is your domain."

"Please." The word forced its way through her lips between pants.

"Please what?" Ian asked and leaned back against the door. "Maybe the little toy in your hot, wet, needy pussy is thinking for you."

Each word pushed every thought between her legs. Her body screamed for release.

"Please. I need to come," Jillian pleaded.

"In actuality, you want to come. You don't need to come. Just like I want to spread you over your beautiful desk and fuck you until you scream my name." The controlled calm belied the strain in the front of his pants, but he didn't move from the door.

"Yes, please," Jillian whispered. The image of her spread out across her own desk raced across her mind.

"Then position yourself face down on your desk. Pull your skirt to your waist. Place your hands on either side of your head and move your feet shoulder width apart. I will take any hesitation in your movement as a lack of consent and we will go to lunch together. Am I clear?"

"Yes, Sir." Jillian nodded her head.

"Then move."

With as much grace as she could muster, Jillian moved across the room to her desk. Her feet moved shoulder width apart as her hands moved the skirt up to her waist. When her hands hit the desk, the vibrator came to life and shot her right to the edge of orgasm.

"Don't you dare come. Your body is mine to control now," Ian said from across the room.

Jillian struggled against the toy's incessant vibration.

"Please, Sir," she begged, but only silence met her plea.

Ian moved behind her. He slipped a finger into the edge of her panties and pushed them to the floor. His hand continued down until it captured the tail of Jillian's vibrating tormentor and pulled it with an excruciating slowness. As soon as it exited her body, it died. Ian set it beside her face to witness her wetness covering it.

Behind her, the quiet rip of foil was the only warning before the condom package hit the desk. Jillian had never felt so turned on. The possibility of being caught added to the excitement between her legs. Ian's hand worked her clit until he finally grabbed her hips and thrust hard into her.

Each stroke was met with a guttural groan as his own need pulsed through her. The sting of his hand caught Jillian by surprise. The sharp spank created a wave of combined pain with pleasure as it rushed through every part of her body. Thrusts met strikes again and again until Jillian lay on her desk in a squirming, panting mess. Each strike was harder than the previous one. Each thrust sent her careening to the edge. Every time his hand connected with her ass, it took her breath away.

"More," Jillian screamed. "Please, Ian, I need more."

His thrusts and spanks became more urgent, forcing them both toward an orgasm which threatened to tear each one apart with its urgency and ferocity.

"IAN!" She screamed his name in desperate need.

"Come for me, Jillian."

Their collective orgasms exploded. Ian continued his relentless pounding. In unison they bucked against each other until their bodies refused to move.

Ian leaned over Jillian's body. For a few minutes they lay there in silence until they caught their collective breath.

They lay there for what felt like an eternity. With effort, Ian guided both of them back to reality and their ability to face the world.

"Shall we go to lunch?" he whispered against her ear as he pulled her body into him.

"After that performance?" Jillian sighed and pulled away enough to straighten her skirt.

"Especially after it. I'm famished." Ian chuckled.

"Lead the way then."

"As often as I can." She heard the smirk in his voice.

In one smooth motion, Ian placed his hand on Jillian's lower back and guided her out of the office. His touch was light, and yet it sent a thrill through her primed body. They walked through the office in silence and paused as she locked up.

Once in the parking garage, he stepped aside and handed her into the car.

Jillian watched him walk in front of the car while the lingering scent of his cologne wrapped around her senses. His head was down, and a frown furrowed his brow as he passed in front of the car. As if he could sense he was being watched, he turned and looked at her, a broad smile reappearing on cue.

He smashed the button on his phone and continued to the driver's side door.

"You look well satisfied." Ian grinned as he slid behind the wheel.

"Then you should look in the mirror." Jillian laughed.

The roar of the engine rumbled the seat. Jillian's heightened senses soaked in each vibration. The internal push and pull of being sensible and the edge of just a little reckless rolled waves of control rolling into the complete need to live in the moment.

"Someone's deep in thought." Ian's voice rumbled through the car as it came to a stop in the valet stand.

"Less thought, more processing what just happened. You looked like something was wrong when we got to the car."

"Nothing that can't be taken care of in a bit on a client's case. Besides, I'd rather focus on the beautiful woman in front of me and the amazing moment that just happened. I thoroughly enjoyed myself." He leaned in to kiss her and paused right before their lips touched.

Jillian's senses ran riot and she pushed forward into his lips.

Their lips met in a kiss that was sensual, possessive, erotic and urgent. He pushed the kiss deeper and Jillian gave up the last thoughts keeping her grounded. For the first time in several years, she felt alive, wanted, and satisfied.

Ian broke the kiss and her eyes flew open to meet his.

"As wonderful as this is, there's no reason to give the valets a show," he said.

A blush bloomed across Jillian's face.

"Um... I guess we should go in."

Ian reached for the door handle, and in time with his movements, both doors opened. As he stepped out, he handed off the keys. The valet handed Jillian out of the car with a smile and a flush of embarrassment rushed through her.

In seconds, Ian was by her side.

"Shall we?" He smiled with a devilishness right on the edges.

CHAPTER TWENTY-FIVE

"Good afternoon, Mr. Breckenridge," the maitre d' said as he looked up from the reservation computer. "We have a table ready for you on the patio, as it is quite a lovely day outside. Will that be satisfactory?"

Ian looked over to Jillian, who smiled and nodded.

"It sounds perfect."

"Right this way, please."

The maitre d' led them through the elegant restaurant and out the patio. Decorated in a style reminiscent of a Parisian bistro, it felt open and airy while maintaining an intimacy.

Ian pulled Jillian's chair out for her as the maitre d' placed the white cloth napkin across her lap. Once settled, Ian moved to sit down across the table.

"Shall I get a bottle of wine from your private collection, Mr. Breckenridge?"

"Please pull the Caymus Napa Valley Cabernet Sauvignon 2016."

"Nice choice, Sir. I'll have your waiter bring it up for you."

"Thank you, François." Ian smirked.

The maitre d' glared at Ian and then smiled as he turned to leave.

"What was all that about?" Jillian asked at the odd exchange.

"We've been friends for years. He goes by Roger, but his formal name is François, after his father. It's always amused me he doesn't go by a name that would be stereotypical for the position."

"Ah, an inside joke." She smiled up at him.

"Yes, and since he ogled my date, I thought it was fair play."

"He was not ogling me."

"Oh yes he was and rightfully so. You're gorgeous. I'm the luckiest man in the restaurant to be accompanied by the most beautiful woman here."

He lowered his gaze to her breasts and smiled in amusement.

Jillian's nipples responded to his gaze, forming hard pebbles underneath her shirt.

"Someone's not playing fair," she whispered.

"Nothing is fair in love and war." A devilish look crossed his face as he grinned.

The waiter arrived at the table and Jillian breathed a sigh of relief.

He was young, somewhere around twenty-six and flashed a boyish grin at Jillian.

"Good evening," he said. "Here is the Caymus Napa Valley Cabernet Sauvignon 2016 you requested, Mr. Breckenridge."

Ian went through ritual as he swirled and tasted the wine before finally nodding.

Wine swished into both glasses an instant later. Once the ritual was complete, the waiter took both orders and turned to leave. The sudden pivot almost made him collide into Edmund. With much apologizing, the waiter stepped around him and headed for the kitchen.

"Dr. Hart, what a pleasant surprise," Edmund said with a smile. When his gaze moved to Ian, it darkened significantly. "I was just on my way to your office."

"Is something wrong?" Jillian asked with concern.

"Quite the opposite, Dr. Hart. I'm heading to Boston on urgent business."

"If you'll excuse me, I need to take care of some business while you two catch up." Ian pulled his phone from his pocket as he rose.

Jillian started to ask a question, but a quick shake of Ian's head made it die on her lips.

"It seems my investment of time and resources is about to pay off handsomely, and they won't even see it coming. Don't you love the thrill of outsmarting the other side, Doctor?"

"That's not exactly the business I'm in, Edmund. I'd much rather help people."

"I know, and you've helped me so much over the years." Edmund smiled.

"That's why it is important for you to know," he said as he bent down until his words whispered into her ear, "I'm sorry, so very sorry."

"Sorry for what?" Jillian looked up, confused.

"Your recent associations will get you hurt if they aren't careful." He smiled down at her. "They are far too concerned with things which are none of their affair."

"Edmund, I don't understand." All of Jillian's training screamed at a problem with the situation, but there was little to indicate any immediate danger. "Why don't you come by my office tomorrow and let's discuss what's going on in your world?"

"I'll schedule time as soon as I get back from Boston. I'll let your office know to cancel all my appointments for the next couple weeks."

"Are you sure this trip can't wait? It seems rushed. Is the business that urgent?" Jillian worked to pull information from him. Something in his demeanor felt off.

"If it weren't important, I wouldn't waste my time with it personally. I look forward to telling you how amazing things turned out when I return. You should know I am sorry, but there was no other way." Without another word, Edmund turned and walked away. Jillian followed his form as he meandered down the sidewalk.

The odd conversation left her unsettled, and she picked up her wine glass for a long pull. Jillian's mind ran over each word to find a message she was sure she'd missed. She swirled her wine and took another long sip to settle her nerves.

"Everthin' d'o... k?" Jillian's words slurred as Ian approached the table.

"Are you okay, Jillian? How many glasses of wine did you drink while I was gone?" He tried to smile but the tone of his voice was full of concern. "Where's Edmund?"

"Heth dong." Jillian shook her head to lift the ever growing fog. Her body wasn't responding and seconds later only a moan passed her lips. Around her she heard a crash, and the world upended.

"What the hell! Jillian!" She saw Ian's body right in front of her, but nothing worked the way her mind commanded it. Around her, chaos took over the scene, but her eyelids were too heavy to take it all in.

"Jillian, stay with me!" Ian commanded, but her head lulled to the side. Her body felt so heavy and tired.

"MOVE!" Ian commanded to the room as he picked up Jillian's limp body and cradled it in his arms.

"Ian, what happened?" Roger appeared at his side.

"I don't know. One minute she was sitting and I thought she'd just had a little too much wine on an empty stomach and the next she's like this."

Roger spoke swiftly into a radio.

"Your car will be out front when you get there. I'll call Angel of Mercy Hospital and tell them you're on your way. It's only 5 blocks from here. She will be okay," Roger tried to assure him.

With the elegance of a bull in a china shop, Ian moved through the restaurant while protecting Jillian's body from the rough movements.

"Please, Jillian, you can't do this to me. I need you," he whispered.

Once outside, he placed Jillian in the car. The valet set her belt while Ian moved to the driver's side. As soon as he was seated, the doors slammed shut and Ian hit the gas.

The five-block drive felt like an eternity. The tires screeched as he wheeled into the emergency dock.

On cue, the medical staff swarmed his car. A doctor shouted orders while nurses bombarded him with questions. Within a few minutes, they wheeled her through a set of doors and out of his sight.

"Sir." The nurse was calling to him, but he wasn't registering the words. "Sir. If you will go park your car and come in, we need to finish filling out paperwork."

With the quiet desperation of a man not used to being out of control, Ian just nodded and climbed back into the car.

CHAPTER TWENTY-SIX

Ian stared at the Jillian's limp body. She'd been out for too long for his preference, but the doctors had assured him she'd be okay. Since he wasn't related to her, it was all the information he'd get from them.

The monitors beside her bed beeped, each one reading out vital information on her current health and well-being. Like a caged panther, he pushed out of his chair and paced the room. In a silent prayer, he called on any deity which came to mind. Every thought swarmed with each event leading them to this hospital room.

What had happened to her and why had he failed to protect her? Worse, he'd almost lost Atlas too. With a network of people working on her case, the one thread they needed had landed in his lap. The minute he'd connected Edmund to Atlas, he'd dialed Kade to warn him of the escalating situation. It sounded like Edmund was inbound and knew where Atlas was hiding. He'd be on a plane right now to back Kade up, but instead he was worried he might lose the most important person in his life.

The phone in his pocket vibrated, and his finger pressed against the screen far harder than necessary.

"Breckenridge."

"Hey, Ian, how's Jillian?" Kade asked from the other end of the line.

"No change." The edge in his voice hid the last vestiges of his crumbling control.

"She will be okay, man."

"That's what they are telling me." Ian sighed. "How are things in Boston?"

"Your team just arrived and Atlas is being evacuated in the next hour. Is there any indication when he'll be on the ground?"

"No. We think he's way ahead of us, though. Our only hope is he doesn't have a specific address, but I don't know for certain."

"Copy that. Don't worry about Atlas, we'll keep her safe. Focus on Jillian, we've got the rest."

"Thanks. Let me know when she's out."

"Will do." Without another word, the line went dead and Ian shoved the phone back in his pocket.

The beep on the monitors changed tempo and Ian's head snapped up to look in response. Jillian moaned from the bed in front of him. In two steps he was by her side.

"Ian," she moaned.

"I'm right here," he said.

"Where am I?" Jillian croaked. Her eyes blinked open and immediately slammed shut against the bright light.

"Angel of Mercy Hospital," Ian replied.

"What happened? Why am I here?"

"They admitted you yesterday afternoon. You collapsed during our lunch."

"My head is killing me. My body hurts," Jillian whispered.

"Ah, you're awake," the doctor said as she passed through the entrance door. "You gave us all quite a scare, Dr. Hart. I'm Dr. Evans. I'll be overseeing your case."

"What's wrong with me?"

Jillian tried to sit up. With a slight shake of her head, she grabbed at the rails on either side of the bed.

"Please, lie back. You've been through quite an ordeal over the last few hours."

Ian reached out and help Jillian settle back into the pillows.

"I've got a few questions for you," Dr. Evans continued as she read from the chart on her tablet. "First, would you like me to request Mr. Breckenridge to leave the room?"

She looked at Ian, then turned a softer look toward Jillian.

"No. Please let him stay."

"Fine. You had quite a combination of powerful drugs in your system. The dosage was just perfect enough not to kill you." Once again the doctor eyed Ian. "The police will be here shortly. They will need to ask you some questions about your associations."

"I need a few minutes, please. This is a lot to process," Jillian whispered.

"Take your time. Just press the button if you need anything. Mr. Breckenridge, will you come out in the hall with me please? The police have questions for you."

Ian nodded.

"Please don't go." Jillian's voice barely rang out over the machines in the room.

He turned and smiled. With a gentle touch, he wiped away the tears under her eyes. "It will be okay. We'll get through this together."

Ian kissed her forehead.

"Let me answer their questions. If you need me, I'm never far away."

With a hesitant step, he turned and followed Dr. Evans out the door.

CHAPTER TWENTY-SEVEN

Tears poured down Jillian's face. Nothing made sense, and every thought felt as if it were being pulled through molasses. The lights in the room hurt her head, but she forced herself through the fog.

A knock at the door startled her out of the emotional onslaught and she swiped at the stream of tears. The sleeve of the blue uniform gave her the only clue to the intruder before the female police officer appeared before her.

"Good afternoon, Dr. Hart. I'm Officer Johnson. Are you up to answering a few questions?" There was a kindness in her voice which rubbed against the command in her presence.

"Of course," Jillian whispered. "I don't know how much help I'll be."

"Let's start with the basics. Can you tell me what happened?" she asked.

For a long minute Jillian stared at her. Did she even know what had happened to her? They said there had been drugs in her system, but it made little sense to her. How did they get there? Who would have drugged her? She was missing something.

"It's all so fuzzy." Jillian swallowed. "One minute..."

"It's okay," the officer reassured her. "Take your time. Let's start with what you remember about the day."

Jillian nodded.

"Ian came by my office to pick me up for lunch." Images of her bent over her desk as he took her from behind bloomed across her memories. Her body reacted unbidden and her breath stuttered.

"Are you okay, Dr. Hart?" the officer asked with concern.

"Yes. It's just all muddled."

"I understand. How long have you known Mr. Breckenridge?" Officer Johnson asked as she jotted down notes on her pad.

"A few weeks."

"How did you two meet?"

"We met at a club. He was part of the security team and we struck up a conversation." Jillian gave the minimum amount of information. There was no reason to suspect Ian would do anything to harm her. He was nothing but a gentleman in every way, and she didn't want to go down that rabbit hole with the police.

"Has he ever abused you or done anything against your will?" The officer deadpanned the question, but it gave away the fact she suspected Ian's involvement and that was not plausible.

"No. He's always very respectful."

"You said he picked you up at your office and took you to lunch. So you didn't come in your own vehicle?"

"No. We rode together."

"Were there any special requests made during lunch?" Officer Johnson asked.

"He requested a bottle of wine from his private collection at the restaurant. It was a very nice bottle of wine based on what I could gather."

"What do you mean based on what you could gather?"

"The maître d' and he were having a conversation about it. They seemed to be friends. From their interaction I gathered it was a nice bottle."

"At any point did he leave the table to go to the bathroom or take a phone call?"

"The waiter poured the wine and Ian tried it. Once he approved it, the waiter poured both glasses. Right after that he stepped away to take a phone call."

"Mr. Breckenridge tried the wine from the bottle?"

Jillian nodded, unsure of why the officer asked these questions.

"Was there anyone else at lunch with you?"

"No. It was just the two of us. Ian reserved the table ahead of time, but I chose the patio. It was a nice day."

The throbbing in Jillian's head pushed the rest of the thoughts back under the undulating fog. Her eyes closed against the onslaught.

"Dr. Hart," Officer Johnson called out.

"I... just need..." The words refused to form as the darkness once again took Jillian and eased her from the nightmare of her world.

CHAPTER TWENTY-EIGHT

Ian looked up as footsteps echoed off the corridor walls.

"Mr. Breckenridge?" The officer inquired with a suspicious as he exited Jillian's hospital room.

"Yes?"

"I need to you come down to the station. We've got a few questions we'd like to go over."

"Do I need a lawyer?" Ian asked in shock.

"That is entirely up to you, Mr. Breckenridge. We want to get your account of the events and think it's best if we do it at the station."

Ian watched Officer Johnson's partner walk up beside her. In a handful of minutes, the entire situation took a turn right before Ian's eyes. One minute he was beside Jillian's bedside, determined to find out what happened. Now he seemed to be facing a different set of problems.

"Am I under arrest?"

"Not at this time, but do not delay in your arrival." The officer gave him a pointed look.

"Understood."

Without further fanfare, the two officers turned and headed toward the elevator.

Ian turned toward Jillian's room, but Dr. Evans stopped him before he could push the door open.

"I'm sorry, Mr. Breckenridge, but you're not allowed in there right now."

None of this made sense. A thousand questions crowded Ian's mind. What had Jillian said to the officer? Had she told them about Edmund? Was he involved? He started toward the elevator but paused mid-stride.

Shit! Edmund. How the hell had he missed it?

Ian reached into his pocket and hit his contact list.

"Kade," came the voice on the other end of the phone.

"It's Ian. Is Atlas extracted?" The relief in his voice was clear.

"Yes. We just finished."

"I need help." Ian's voice shook, and he admonished himself for his moment of weakness.

"What's wrong?" Concern filled Kade's voice. "Is Jillian okay?"

"Yes, but I think I'm about to get arrested."

"What? What's going on?"

"I'm not sure. An officer interviewed Jillian and when they came out, they told me to come down to the station."

"Then what makes you think you're about to get arrested?"

"I overheard the nurses saying Jillian's lab work just came back. I caught a couple of the drugs they listed off. It was worse than any date rape cocktail. She was out to lunch with me. These cases never go far from the obvious."

"And you left the table to call me about Atlas."

"Yes." Ian sighed as the pieces fell into place.

"Didn't you say Edmund was at the restaurant?"

"Yes. But he was gone by the time I arrived back at the table. Jillian's speech was slurred as I came back, and I thought she'd just had too much wine. Then she collapsed and the world's been chaos since."

"Do you think Edmund knew we were on to him?"

"No. Maybe. I don't know. But mostly he ignored me. He walked up to the table to talk to Jillian. She seemed to know him."

"Friends? Or patient?"

"I don't know. What am I missing and how did I miss it?" Ian swore under his breath.

"Let's take it one problem at a time. Atlas is safe for now. I'll get Samantha back over to the hospital to stay with Jillian and have her call the club's lawyer on the way."

"I'll call my..." Ian started but Kade interrupted.

"Listen, man, I've already missed too much not being able to protect Atlas from Edmund. Especially since I was there right after he proposed. I've got this one. Besides, it's on Atlas' account." Kade tried to lighten up the situation with a little humor.

"Thanks, man."

"Don't thank me yet. There's still a lot of moving pieces on this board and we are way behind the game play," Kade said and the line went dead.

Ian pushed his hands through his hair and headed out of the hospital in the opposite direction of his desire.

CHAPTER TWENTY-NINE

Jillian forced her eyes open. Her body demanded the comfort of sleep, but she knew consciousness was more important. The incessant beep of monitors gave her something to focus on until she forced herself out of the murky depths.

"I hope someone got the number of that bus," she quipped without opening her eyes.

"I believe they are getting close to that one." Samantha's voice rang through the room.

"Why do you sound so worried? I'm not dead." Jillian tried to laugh, but it came out as a hoarse moan.

Beside her, she heard Samantha inhale deeply.

"The last couple of days have been trying," she finally said.

Jillian forced her eyes open to get a good look at her best friend.

"What aren't you telling me?" Jillian said and quirked an eyebrow.

"You look like hell," Samantha said with a forced smile.

"It matches how I feel. Now tell me what's going in the world- and where's Ian?"

"He's a little tied up right now."

"The bigger question is why are you being evasive?" Jillian

grabbed the bed rails and quickly pulled herself upright. Immediately she regretted the motion when her stomach revolted in a fit of nausea.

"You need rest. The last two days were not easy on you."

"Two days?! What do you mean two days? I've got patients to see. Wait- why is Ian tied up right now?"

Samantha's look was pure pity. Jillian hated that look. Aimed at her she despised it even more.

"They have arrested him. They think he did this to you. They said there was evidence of sex and charged him with sexual assault, but they are reviewing it for heavier charges."

The words climbed through Jillian's brain, demanding her to understand. She willed her mind to focus on what Samantha wasn't explicitly saying. With excruciating slowness, the concepts formed.

"Wait. They think Ian did this? That's not right. Nothing about it is right. Why would he drug me after consensual sex?" The words spilled out of Jillian's mouth without thought. "I'm missing something. It's like knowing... a word on the tip of the tongue... but the memory is just not there. This is frustrating!" Jillian screamed.

A crash made Samantha's head jerk up to see two nurses and a doctor rush through the door.

"Dr. Hart, you need to calm down." The machine beside her beeped at a rapid staccato. Her heart thundered in rapid rhythm. Each breath was more labored than the last. Panic swirled through her.

"I... can't... calm... down," Jillian panted. "Where's Ian?"

"Mr. Breckenridge is indisposed," the nurse replied quietly. "You need to calm down."

An oxygen mask covered her face in the next minute.

"Deep breaths, Dr. Hart," the nurse coached.

"He... didn't... do anything... wrong," Jillian pleaded. Unbidden tears ran down the side of her face.

"As a professional, we are often the last to realize the realities of an abusive relationship," the nurse started.

"He didn't... he wasn't."

"The bruises on your body, the evidence collected while you were unconscious, and your current state would suggest otherwise," Dr. Evans hissed.

Jillian shook her head and looked at Samantha with pleading eyes.

"It will be okay, Jillian. Kade sent Atlas' lawyer to help Ian. You need to get through this first, or you can't help him." Samantha's voice was firm. Each word was full of unsaid information.

Even though Jillian couldn't comprehend it, she knew one thing-the only way to help Ian was to get the hell out of here.

CHAPTER THIRTY

Ian took a deep breath as he walked through the door.

"You don't realize the value of freedom..." Images of Jillian in various bound positions came to his mind.

"... Until you've lost it, even for a minute." John gave him a knowing smile.

"It provides a fresh perspective on things, for sure," Ian agreed with a nod.

"I'm glad Kade called me. They were trying to build a case against you. The evidence is flimsy, but Jillian's missing memories aren't helping your case."

"True, but the restaurant full of witnesses will. Did you call Roger and ask him about the waiter? He ran into Edmund as he approached the table." Ian continued to walk at an increasing rapid pace down the police station stairs.

"My office is already in contact with him. Do you think this Edmund person drugged Jillian?" John asked, concern lacing his voice.

"Yes," Ian stated and slid into the limousine.

John slid in after him and gave instructions to the driver.

"Care to elaborate?" John finally asked.

Ian let out a long breath.

"Atlas was missing because Edmund was stalking her, but she never told her security. He'd proposed to her after a session but didn't take the rejection well. None of the pieces were falling into place. In addition, he's one of Dr. Hart's patients."

"That's quite a picture you're painting. Are you saying Edmund is behind the drugging of Dr. Hart?"

"That's my belief." Ian shook his head. "I just don't know why we took so long to put all the pieces together."

He slammed his fist into the seat in front of him.

"Careful. Alexandra won't take kindly to mistreatment of her car." John gave a wry smile.

"No, Atlas would hate it," Ian agreed.

"Do you think her duplicity caused the delay in putting together what was going on?"

"It probably contributed to it, but I can't blame her for doing it. She's a powerful woman in DC where the politics of the day can make one of her professions safe in one minute and dangerous the next. Especially when those same politicians are clients."

"True," John stated.

Both men fell into silence as they drove through the city. Twenty minutes later, the car came to a stop in front of an office building in Rosslyn. John's door opened, and he turned to Ian.

"This mess will take a few weeks to clean up. I'd advise you to limit certain proclivities until then. While they were releasing you, I got a call that Jillian is out of the hospital, but they've taken a temporary restraining order against you on her behalf. Please don't go see her for a couple days. That includes all forms of contact. It's in your best interest."

"This is absurd!"

"Absurd or not, it is the position you are in right now. Let me do my job and don't make it harder on me or when Alexandra is back, I'll tell her what a pain in the ass you were during her absence."

Ian nodded at the attempt to lighten the mood.

"That threat's enough to bring almost anyone to heel."

"I hope so," John said as he exited the car. "I'll be in touch. Stay out of trouble."

CHAPTER THIRTY-ONE

Jillian paced her office. The world made little sense. When the drugs had been flushed out of her system, the hospital released her. Everything in her knew Ian would come see her, but every text and call went unanswered. The more she tried to make sense of the last two weeks, the further from the answers she seemed to wander.

Samantha was a rock of support. She'd told Jillian about the situation with Alexandra and the fact someone was stalking her. However, no matter how much she pried, Samantha wouldn't give her the details. It was always a tragedy when someone obsessed over another person to the point of possession. Restless, she moved back to her desk and tried to focus on the paperwork cluttering her workspace.

On the recommendation of the doctors and her colleagues, her schedule was clear of patients for at least two more weeks. If she didn't go crazy first.

The knock on her door startled her out of her thoughts.

"Come." Jillian worked to keep her tone even and in command.

She looked over to see who was interrupting her unproductive afternoon. As if on cue, Jacob White walked through the door, concern etched on his face.

"I'm glad to see the rumors of your demise were exaggerated," he quipped.

"Quite." Jillian forced a smile and nodded.

"It's good to see you up and around. The board asked me to check in on you and see if I would recommend filling up your schedule again."

"Excellent. I'm feeling great. No physical side effects. Easy evaluation. Tell them I can get back to work immediately." She stood up from her desk and walked to the front. "As you can see, everything is in order and I'm right as rain."

Jacob chuckled. "Steamrolling me will never work, and you know it. Shall we take a seat so I can ask you a few questions?"

"Can I get you a cup of coffee?" Jillian asked with a sweet tone.

"That would be fabulous, but it will not derail me from asking the necessary questions."

"We can get to those soon. Patience is a wonderful gift." She busied herself with the two coffee mugs and the almost permanently filled carafe, thanks to her efficient assistant. When she could not stall any longer, she walked the coffee service over to the sitting area. Jacob sat in the chair she normally took. With a huff, she sat down on the sofa reserved for her patients.

A smile quirked on the edge of Jacob's lips at her frustration.

"You know, the sooner you answer my questions, the sooner I'll get out of your hair and you can get on with your life," he said in a tone shaped by far too many advanced degrees and edged with years of friendship.

"Fine." Jillian huffed and let her eyes close. Around her the silence was deafening. When she once again opened them, Jacob sat there staring at her. She knew the look of evaluation. The one when you're trying to decide what someone is hiding and if it is important.

"Tell me what you remember about your lunch out with Ian," Jacob stated.

"Yes, Dr. White, by all means let's jump into the deep end." Her response dripped with sarcasm.

"Jillian, I'm not here to hurt you."

"I know. But I've answered that same inquiry more times than I care to count over the last two weeks."

"Then one more won't be so bad."

"It's simple. Ian and I went to lunch. He talked to his friend Roger who seated us. He ordered wine from his private collection. After he tasted it, he stepped away to take a phone call. Then everything is a blur," Jillian recounted in clipped tones. "They arrested Ian, but I have few details on the reason. Samantha said the club's attorney is representing him and she isn't allowed to discuss it."

"I see." Jacob scribbled quick notes on a small pad in his lap. "How many glasses of wine did you drink while Mr. Breckenridge was away from the table?"

"I don't remember even finishing one. Maybe a long sip, two at the most, but I can't be certain."

"Tell me about the other people in the restaurant," Jacob continued.

"You want me to tell you about the other people in the restaurant?" Jillian replied with exasperation.

"Yes, please."

"How do you expect me to know anything about the people in the restaurant?"

"The longer you evade the questions, the longer this will take, Jillian. You observe people for a living."

"The reservation was for an inside table, but it was beautiful outside. So we went out to the patio. My focus was on Ian. Everything in me buzzed after the most amazing..." Jillian's words faded and a flush crawled up her face.

"The most amazing what, Jillian?"

"Um." The memories of her spread over her desk made her adjust on the sofa. Twice she crossed then uncrossed her legs. Ian had commanded her body in ways she'd not experienced. The mere thought of him made her want to follow the next words out of his mouth.

"Jillian?"

"Sorry. I was just trying to remember what happened earlier in the day."

"Trying? It looked like you were succeeding." Jacob smiled. "Let me bring you back to the restaurant."

"Yes. The restaurant. Have you ever had an experience where the memory feels just out of reach? You know it's right there but you can't bring it close enough?"

Jacob nodded but let Jillian continue.

"It is as if the memory is right there, but time jumps from Ian leaving the table to take a phone call to the hospital."

A long silence swirled between them.

"I might be able to help if you are willing," Jacob said.

"What did you have in mind, Dr. White?"

"Hypnosis."

"Hypnosis? That's your brilliant solution?" Jillian scoffed.

"You said it yourself, Jillian, the memory is right there. I know you prefer traditional talk therapy in your practice, but I've found hypnosis can get people over the edge. A block, if you will. You're in control of the entire process. There's nothing I'm saying right now you don't know."

"Okay."

The whisper was so soft it barely moved the air.

"Was that consent to proceed?" Jacob asked.

"Yes," Jillian said with more confidence. "I need to know what happened. My life is this cycle of people I trust, let them intimately in and then end up in terrible situations. If Ian did this to me, then my cycle of poor choices continues, and if it wasn't him, then I want to know why I ended up in the hospital on a drug cocktail that almost killed me."

"There you are, Dr. Hart. Welcome back to the fight." Jacob smiled.

Jillian set her cup down on the coffee table.

"Take off your shoes and rest your feet flat on the floor. Just relax. We are just going to talk. You are in the lead on where we go," he said. "Rest your hands comfortably on your thighs and let yourself follow my words. Nothing matters outside of this space.

"Take a deep breath in... exhale letting the worries and cares go... unwind completely... relaxing more and more... as soon as a thought forms... it drifts away... Breathe in... and as you breathe out... relax and let your eyes close."

Jillian followed the steady rhythm of Jacob's voice as it moved from a conversational tempo to a much slower pace. With each slowing of the words, she found herself more focused on them until they were all that mattered.

"More and more comfortable... as you go down... more relaxed with each word... muscles limp and relaxed... drifting deeper and deeper... tension drains out... waves of relaxation... roll over your body... and it becomes more relaxed... your mind follows... my voice... drifting... deeper down... feeling completely at peace... calm and content... safe and secure... my voice takes you deeper... more relaxed and open."

The last vestige of tension washed across Jillian's body. His words took her to a state of peace she hadn't experienced in a long time.

"Jillian... as you go deeper and deeper... I want you... to see the restaurant... feel the breeze... across your skin... tell me what you see."

"A patio. Ian is across from me. A man and woman at a table in the corner. Two women laughing, drinking martinis."

"Excellent... let those images take you deeper down... with each image... you relax... more and more. Do you see anyone else?"

"The waiter is pouring wine. A glass is in front of Ian. The waiter runs into a man."

"You are doing well... here you are safe... fall deeper into this place... do you see the man and the waiter?"

"Yes."

"Describe the man."

"He is tall. In a suit..." Jillian's words stopped. The rate of her breath picked up and Jacob sat forward in his chair.

"You are safe, Jillian... relax... take a deep breath... let the fresh air... fill you and contentment spreads..." He watched her body as it relaxed back into the sofa and her breathing returned to a slow pace. "My voice keeps you safe... move deeper and deeper... the man cannot harm you here... Do you know the man?"

"No..." Jillian paused. "Yes?"

"Who is the man, Jillian?"

"I can't see his face. He's talking to me."

"What is he saying?"

"He's sorry. I will be hurt. He's sorry."

"Where is Ian, Jillian?"

"He's not here. I can see him at the entrance of the restaurant."

"That's good... the breeze moves across your skin... you hear a man's voice... is the voice loud?"

"It is a whisper."

"This is a voice you've heard before?"

"Yes."

"Is it the voice of a friend?"

"No."

"Is it the voice of a colleague?"

"No."

"A staff member?"

"No. I don't know." Frustration edged Jillian's voice.

"It is okay... follow my voice... relax and step deeper down... just let it come to you... the more you relax... the easier it flows... and the easier it flows... the more you relax."

Jillian inhaled deeply and settled back into the seat.

"Let the voice come to you... it is a familiar voice... one you have heard before... where have you heard it?"

"My office." The words tumbled out.

"Very good... you are doing so well... the voice was heard in your office."

"Yes."

An image formed in Jillian's mind. Edmund sat on the sofa across from her. He was late to an appointment. Something unusual for him. "I'm so sorry for my tardiness, Dr. Hart."

The two voices collided in her mind. "Edmund! OMG! The voice was Edmund's."

"Is Edmund a patient?"

"Yes!"

Tears streamed down Jillian's face as the memory flooded her mind. Edmund leaned down and threatened her. She was shaken when he left and took two large gulps of her wine to settle her nerves.

"Jillian..." Jacob's urgent voice cut through the waves threatening to take her under. "You are safe... my voice is your anchor... follow my words... they are a place of safety."

He continued to guide her until she once again relaxed.

"It's almost time to come back... as you come back... you'll notice you are becoming more aware of my voice... the more aware you become... the more energy you feel... everyday thoughts float back into your mind... it's time to come out of trance... in a few minutes... when you are ready... you will feel refreshed and alert... more and more alert... energetic and active... aware of my voice. Open your eyes, Jillian."

Jillian opened her eyes and stared at Jacob.

"It's okay, Jillian, you're safe here."

He walked over to the side table and poured her a glass of water. Without a word, he handed it to her. She nodded in acknowledgement and he returned to his seat.

Jacob steepled his fingers in front of him and watched as Jillian resettled into the present. After a few sips of water, she looked up with caution.

"Who's Edmund, Jillian?"

"He's a patient. I consulted you on him."

"Why would he want to drug you in a public place? It is dramatic and distracting."

"He's obsessed. Until just now, none of it made sense." Jillian shook her head at the thoughts running through it.

"Words. Outside ones," Jacob commanded gently. "I'm here to help, but I can only do it if you let me in."

Jillian nodded but took a few minutes to collect her own understanding.

"Edmund is a patient of mine. He is obsessed over a woman. A friend of mine had a friend go missing recently. She never gave me the details. Edmund told me at the restaurant he was going to Boston. My friend said the woman who was missing was evacuated from Boston. It's related somehow."

Jacob listened without comment.

"I'm still missing something, but whatever that piece is, it is the reason he drugged me."

"Looks like Ian is in the clear," Jacob stated.

"Oh my God. They think Ian drugged me!"

"Looks like you need to go clear up the issue."

Jillian jumped up from the sofa, slipped her feet into her shoes, and hustled to her desk.

"Are you okay to drive?" Jacob asked.

"Yes and thank you."

"I'm glad I could help. Once you clear Ian, let's discuss your patient."

Jillian nodded and headed for the door.

CHAPTER THIRTY-TWO

Ian stared at the desk in front of him. Behind it, John spoke on the phone in clipped sentences. He scrubbed his face with his hand and looked up at the sound of the receiver hitting the phone base.

"That was an interesting call. They dropped the charges against you. They even sent along an apology. It seems Dr. Hart recovered her memory and went to the police station to straighten out the confusion. According to the police chief, that woman is a force of nature. She dressed him down for leading questions when she was in a drugged state." John chuckled.

"So it's over?" Hesitation laced Ian's voice.

"Yes, Mr. Breckenridge, it is over."

"Please call me Ian, we've gone over this."

"Indeed. I understand we have you to thank for getting Alexandra out of her predicament."

"Kade did the heavy lifting. My team just provided information and infrastructure. Speaking of forces of nature, a woman who can keep up that many masks is one."

"An accurate statement. I'm very disappointed she didn't confide in her own team when things hit the fan." John leaned back in his chair.

"Fear will do strange things to people, when they can protect the people they love."

"Indeed," Ian acknowledged, thoughts of Jillian and her own fierce loyalty pouring through him.

"Now get out of here. I believe you need to go express your thanks in the most appropriate ways." John smiled.

"It makes me wonder how you define appropriate."

John chuckled. "You've got a good imagination. I'm sure you'll figure it out."

Ian smiled. "Send your bill to my office."

"Not on your life. Alexandra's got this one. She owes you and the BMW payments she covers is due."

"Ah- lawyer jokes. Don't quit your day job." Ian laughed and turned on his heel.

He pulled the phone out of his pocket as he headed out the door. Every text and missed call made him feel guilty, but he knew John's advice had kept him out of further legal trouble. Except it hurt the one person he'd promised never to abandon. Guilt covered him. He would never forgive himself for the pain he'd caused her, but he damn sure would spend the rest of his life making it up to her. If she would let him.

His fingers moved deftly over the keyboard.

You are amazing and beautiful. Please forgive me.

Ian hit send on the text message and headed to his car. Each second felt like an eternity. To his surprise, the phone vibrated in his pocket as he approached the driver's door.

Meet me at the club at 6pm. There is a reserved room. I think a public private space is best.

The simple message deflated the earlier elation. The words brought him to his knees, but he climbed into his car, prepared to meet the fate created for him.

CHAPTER THIRTY-THREE

Jillian stared at the empty private room. The memory of their last time here skittered across her thoughts, making the butterflies in her stomach declare war on one another. With practiced effort, she stepped to the sideboard and poured a glass of water. A bottle of wine, a Caymus Napa Valley Cabernet Sauvignon 2016, sat beside the water carafe. Fear threatened to pull her under and take hold.

"For God's sakes, Jillian, it's just a bottle of wine," she admonished herself out loud.

Her eyes raked across the two sparkling wine glasses. The bottle brought back the nuances of the waking nightmare she'd walked through in the last two weeks. With several deep breaths, she settled her nerves and picked up the water glass.

The room felt vast with all the equipment pushed against the wall. On her right, the throne chair loomed. The push pull of control forced against her ragged emotions. A glance at her watch told her time was running short. In the next few moments her world would go only one of two ways, and right now she didn't know which way she wanted more.

Jillian moved toward the throne. Her hand brushed over the soft velvet fabric, then pushed it the opposite way until its softness turned rigid under her hand. In every way it was perfect. With a flare of confidence she didn't internalize, she turned and sat upon the throne and waited.

At exactly six o'clock, the door opened, and Ian entered. The minute his eyes met hers, they bored straight to her soul. The intense gaze screamed the rolling storm moving through him.

She broke the gaze before she backed out of her plan, but not before she saw Ian's recognition of the bottle beside him.

"Jillian," he whispered.

"Don't!" she interrupted. "Don't walk in here with excuses and platitudes. Don't tell me how it will be different this time. How you won't abandon me for weeks."

Jillian closed her eyes to steel herself against her own words. Each thrown dagger stabbed her own heart deeper. When she needed him the most he hadn't been there. The facts were simple. Once again, she'd let herself fall. And once again she was alone in her darkest hours.

Her gaze trailed Ian as he approached her. His muscles rippled with tension as he strode across the floor. The emotions playing across his face were pure ferocity mixed with an odd tenderness. When he arrived in front of her, he stood in silence. The sheer command of his presence caused her breath to catch. Under his heavy stare, she felt the weight on her as much as if he'd physically tied her to it. Beneath his shirt, the ripple of his muscles were the only sign of his own emotions.

They sat there. The first one to flinch would lose this stand-off. The war of stubborn pride and need to give in to their connection battled in the air. Jillian's breath became rapid inhales. Her entire being called out to him, but she refused to lose her heart to a man who would throw her away at the first sign of a problem.

"You're in my chair." He spoke the words with evenness and authority, which belied the fact it was just above a whisper.

The words snapped the last vestiges of Jillian's control. Her body moved under its own volition as she leaped up from her seat. The water glass crashed to the floor. With it, the mastery of her emotion shattered.

Fear pushed her to take a step back, but the simple fact was she didn't want this to end. He was everything she needed. She wanted him in her life. Her body screamed for a decision. Her emotions told her to jump. Logic dictated he'd not contacted her for noble reasons. Only fear screamed at her to walk away.

Her lips curled in a smile. She was still here because this was where she belonged. They would work past fears and boundaries together.

"Master me, Ian." The word cut through the tension like a razor-sharp knife.

"With pleasure, Jillian."

With controlled confidence, he tore open the condom packet he'd snagged from his pocket.

"Put it on." He handed it to Jillian, his eyes never leaving hers.

Her hands shook as she loosened his belt. With the slightest trepidation, she pulled down the zipper of his pants to relieve him from the confines of the fabric.

Jillian leaned back and slowly rolled the rubber over his cock. The action was met with a groan of pleasure at her touch. His deep pants proved he struggled with control along with her.

"Strip." The simple command sent her careening back toward the edge.

Without grace, she stripped out of her clothes. From the corner of her eye, she watched Ian do the same.

In the next instance, Jillian was lifted and straddling his lap. He cupped her face, taking advantage of her open mouth and controlling her in a way that made her heart dance. His tongue took over, circling around hers before thrusting deep.

Jillian eased her hips into the air and slid over his hard cock.

"You will fuck yourself hard on my cock." His thickness pulsed inside her.

"Yes, Ian." Her voiced sat right above a whisper.

She arched and clenched, her body moving up and down on his cock. Each thrust pierced her until it buried deep inside her. Ian's face twisted in pleasure and amazement. Unspoken questions passed in a look between them, but doubt scattered to the four winds.

"Yes," Jillian screamed. Her body moved in an abandonment she had never experienced. Both controlled and in control.

"Amazing," Ian whispered. His control hung on the edge.

She arched her back until his cock sat just at her entrance, then plunged back down in sharp distinct movements.

"Look at me," Ian commanded.

The sharp order cut through the air. Jillian's eyes flew open. Passion filled her look, and he returned it with the same expression, pinched right on the edge of orgasm.

"Come for me."

Jillian screamed as he met her thrusts with hard ones of his own. She bucked on him, her back arching in release, and felt him shutter his own orgasm beneath hers in response. Her thrusts slowed, and she collapsed forward onto Ian's chest and he pulled her closer. Wrapped around him, she felt like they were one.

JILLIAN OPENED HER MOUTH TO RETORT TO HIS REMARK. THEY still had to talk, but it could wait. He needed to be in her, now. It had been too long, and actions spoke louder than words.

His lips covered hers before the words slipped past, crushing over them with authority. The desperate battle played out when his tongue entered her mouth. He tasted like the sweetest chocolate, and her starved senses surrendered to his onslaught. Ian owned the kiss and Jillian was helpless to do anything but follow his lead.

His firm lips demanded everything from her. Everything in her mind softened, thoughts dissipated, and her head spun with desire. She reached for him, like an anchor in a sudden storm, grasping his arms in a failing effort to stay grounded.

Ian's fingers threaded through the soft tendrils of her hair. She moaned at the sensation. The dam of pent-up need burst through her. He met each parry and thrust of her tongue. His hand fisted in her hair and pulled until the pain made her flinch. For a fleeting second he broke the kiss.

"Touch me," he ground out.

Instantly her hands reached out and pulled at the buttons of his shirt. In the next moment they flew across the room as the tedium frustrated her need to touch him. Her hands wandered down to his waist, undoing his pants and reaching inside, closing around his hard cock.

Ian pulled back. Both gasped for breath. He pushed up her top and let his fingers explore her breasts. The pert buds stood taut under his ministrations as if begging for more. Leaning forward, he devoured the left one as his teeth scraped against over sensitized skin.

Jillian moaned and pulled away. He clamped down his teeth in response and she cried out under his sudden attack.

"Ian," Jillian panted. "I need you."

She resumed caressing his cock. The firm, slow strokes soothed over his soft skin. His cock grew, straining toward her, as he arched his hips and thrust his cock into her fist, grunting his own need in response.

He leaned forward and clamped his teeth hard on her shoulder, locking her in place. Marking what was his. In response, Jillian tilted her neck to give him more room.

"Mine," he growled when he let go of her shoulder to reclaim her mouth.

Jillian's body was an inferno sitting on the edge of ignition. He moved his hands down between her legs and she nearly exploded. His fingers circled her clit.

A moan pushed against the onslaught of his lips. Her hips thrust into his touch and his fingers slid into her.

"Please, Ian. I'm going to come," Jillian begged against his lips.

Ian ripped his lips from hers.

"No, Jillian. You know the rules." He pushed her hand away from his cock and groaned.

His fingers continued the work through her wetness. Her eyes felt heavy as he pushed her closer to the edge, only to rip her back from it.

"You're mine." Jillian held his gaze, wanting to believe his words. "Tell me you understand."

She wiggled her hips, searching for what he withheld. Her wetness coated his hand as she pushed against it.

"Please, Ian," she begged.

"No. Not until you tell me you understand."

Jillian's body stilled.

"Trust me." His finger ran along the wet hot opening of her pussy.

Her head tilted forward until it pressed against his. Her breaths moved in gusts and pants. She knew he was pushing her. Logically he'd done everything necessary to protect her, but fear fought with logic and need.

"Trust me, Jillian. You belong to me," he whispered.

The heavy air hung around them. A point of no return hung on the simplest words.

CHAPTER THIRTY-FOUR

Jillian woke in a cloud of the softest blankets she'd ever known. The smell of food pulled on her senses until she gave in and opened her eyes. The small private club room was transformed around her. In the center of the room, a well-adorned table sat with one place setting. Beside it a trolly of food perched temptingly.

Ian sat upon the throne reading a book. His pressed clothes showed no signs of their earlier encounter. When she stirred, he looked from his book and down at her. A smile crept across his face.

"Hello, beautiful." The low timbre of his voice rumbled through his chest. "I ordered food."

It was a statement. His calm command and control eased the mantle of sleep from her body.

"It smells amazing," Jillian replied.

"Join me?" he asked as he stood, placing the book on the seat and outstretching his hand toward her.

With a nod, she reached for him and let him help her stand. The blankets fell away to reveal her naked form in contrast with his covered one. A flush crept across her body and she lowered her hands to hide it slightly.

"Don't hide from me, Jillian." The admonishment was soft, but the look in his eyes demanded obedience.

With a deep inhale, she dropped her hands. It would take time to get used to being so open again.

"Come." He motioned toward the table. When they approached the table, he turned to her. "Kneel."

Jillian hesitated. Their last meal together had ended in her almost dying in the middle of a public restaurant. As she stood in front of him, in the most vulnerable way possible, the fear rushed toward her at the speed of a bullet train.

"Trust me, Jillian. I've got you." Ian's calm voice stroked against the raging fear.

Finally, she let her body fold toward the floor.

"Beautiful." His praise filled her, but she still felt at sea.

"I'm scared." The words slipped past her lips.

"I know. We will walk through this fear together," Ian said. His calm, steady voice created a path for her to follow out of her drowning emotions. "There will be things here to face your nightmare, but we'll get through it."

Jillian nodded at words that made little sense and worked to relax beside him.

Above her, he cut food on his plate and fed it to her by hand. The odd situation sent a thrill through her. As the meal progressed, an easy conversation arose. Each of them kept the topics light. The lilt of her laughter rang across the room, and Ian smiled down at her.

"Drink," he commanded and handed her a glass of wine.

Jillian froze without taking the glass from him.

"It's a beautiful wine, Jillian. Don't let the fear take away the pleasure. This wine is rich and fruity across the palate with just a hint of flavors from dark berries." His words were just noises in the air.

The rich dark liquid swirled about the glass in her shaking hands. She'd bought the bottle to replace the one in his collection. Now the memories of the last time it had crossed her palate threatened to take her under.

"It's safe, Jillian. I promise. Don't let that monster take away your pleasure," Ian said and pushed away from the table. In a graceful motion, he sank to his knees in front of her. "You are the heart of my heart. The very soul which keeps me alive. May I give back to you what he took from us?"

Jillian looked up into Ian's pleading eyes. Tears trickled down her face and his thumb wiped them away. Her body shook with fear, but she needed to get past this if they were to move forward. Silently she nodded.

"Words, Jillian. I need your words. Do you trust me enough to follow me wherever I lead?"

Only the lightest lilt of the background music punctured the edge of the silence held between them.

"I don't know how to get through this, but I trust you."

"We get through it together."

To punctuate the words, Ian cupped his hands under hers and brought the wine glass to his lips. He tilted it toward him and let the wine fill his mouth to prove it was safe. Jillian stared at him in anticipation.

Ian took the glass from her and set it on the table. He leaned forward and wound his hand through her hair, pulling her head backwards. Her mouth opened in response and he covered it with his as he fed her the wine.

The warm liquid flooded her mouth. She barely tasted it, as it scoured her throat. Ian pulled her into his arms. The pent-up emotions of the last two weeks rushed out in a heart-wrenching sob.

"I've got you, beautiful. You're safe," Ian repeated. "I love you, Jillian."

CHAPTER THIRTY-FIVE

Ian perched against the low wall running along the rooftop terrace of the Empyrean Club. He stared out over the paddocks surrounding the property. The sounds of laughter and splashing water resonated up from the pool below. The cloudless sky and warm sun made him feel more hopeful than he'd felt in months. A soft breeze tousled his hair as he gazed out across the open land. Around him, a burst of laughter from Samantha and Jillian brought his attention back to his surroundings. A smile crossed his face. For the first time in months, the world was going in the right direction.

"Being antisocial?" Kade said, the thump of his boots across the roof alerting Ian to his presence before he spoke.

"Nah. Just enjoying the moment," Ian replied as he turned.

Kade handed him a scotch glass.

"Thanks. How are things at the club?"

"Different, but we're finding our rhythm for now. I'm just glad Alexandra's safe." Dark sunglasses covered Kade's eyes, but an easiness settled across his body.

"She will be okay," Ian reassured him. "I hear you're training Cassandra."

Kade nearly choked on his beer. "Wow, the grapevine works fast around here."

"In this community? It's more like wildfire." Ian chuckled.

"There's an understatement. Things are... different." His voice held a touch of uncertainty.

"You've got this. I hear she gives you a run for your money."

"Yeah, just what I need, another challenging woman in my life." Kade rolled his eyes.

"Those are the best type." Ian grinned. "Speaking of..."

"Go. And thanks again."

"Enough of that nonsense," Ian replied. "I've always got your six."

Ian turned and scanned the crowd. He already knew where Jillian was without looking. As he approached, she shot him a smile. Her fingers fidgeted with the necklace around her throat. A reminder when the world sent her astray. They'd gone through a couple of emotional days as Jillian worked through her own fears, but every day she got better, and he loved her strength.

He dragged her to him and kissed her deeply. Jillian opened to him, giving back everything she took. Her eyes were filled with a soft contentment he hoped would never leave. In his arms, she melted.

"Hey you." She grinned up at him when he finally released her.

"Hey yourself. Are you behaving yourself?"

"Jillian?" Samantha rolled her eyes. "She's nothing but trouble."

"Just the way I like her," Ian quipped back.

"Good thing, because I hear she's trying to corrupt Cassandra."

"I am not," Jillian protested. "She's already corrupted."

The three of them laughed.

"You doing okay?" Ian whispered against her ear, noting the wine glass in her hand.

"Better now." She smiled up at him. The trust she'd shown in him made his heart swell. With each step Jillian let down her guard and the hints of vulnerability overpowered him.

Ian kissed the edge of her temple. "I love you."

Jillian pressed against him.

"I love you, Ian. Master of me." Her voice was firm but just above a whisper.

Samantha smiled over at the pair.

"Get a room you two. Or better yet, go play downstairs so we can watch."

A flush crept over Jillian when others chimed in with a chorus of, "Yes, please."

Behind her, laughter rumbled through Ian's chest. She was right where she belonged.

EPILOGUE

The click of the keyboard was the only sound in the room. Computer screens flickered in the dim light. Voices emanated from the speakers until they were a jumble of words.

"Dr. Hart, Mr. Breckenridge is here to see you."

"Send him in," the female voice sang through the chatter.

With a keystroke, all the other voices stopped.

"Hello, beautiful." A male voice vibrated across the speakers.

"Hello yourself."

The sound of an intimate kiss filled the room.

"Since your schedule is full, I brought a picnic," the male voice said.

"How thoughtful. Thank you, Ian."

"I promised to protect you and take care of you."

"I can feed myself," Jillian said.

"And yet you forget to do it so often." Ian laughed.

The rustle of bags and paper let the listener know they were laying out lunch.

"Have you heard from Alexandra?"

"I got an update this morning. They are all settled in the villa."

"Mmm... The Caribbean waters and a trade wind. I know she's in hiding, but that's not a bad place to hide," Jillian replied.

"I believe a fear for one's life might put a damper on the environment."

"Or raise the intensity of the interaction. Bondage and a little fear are an aphrodisiac."

"Is that a request I hear, my dear?"

"When this mess is over, I'm all for a little adventure to that same little villa in St. Kitt. Seclusion, sun, and sand would do me some good."

He hit the volume on the speaker and picked up the phone.

"Good afternoon, how can we help you today, Sir?"

"Please book a private plane to St. Kitts. Round trip. Wheels up in two hours."

"Yes, Sir."

Edmund clicked off the phone and immediately dialed the next number.

"Please make accommodation arrangements for a villa on St. Kitts for two months with the ability to extend."

He listened to the acknowledgement and answered the questions. Once the arrangements were made, he leaned back in his chair.

"I'm coming for you, Alexandra. Soon you will be all mine."

He lifted a glass toward his monitor.

"Thank you, Dr. Hart, for your help. I knew those bugs would pay off. So much leverage over so many people. Who knew your clientele was so powerful? Profitable indeed."

Edmund turned up the volume on Dr. Hart's office.

"Ian!" Jillian mocked an admonishment. "I don't think this is what they mean when they tell people I'm tied up."

"Maybe it should be." Ian laughed. "I bet you'd look beautiful tied to the mast of a sailboat."

"What a perverted mind you have, Master of me."

"Only for you, my dear. Only for you."

PLEA FROM THE AUTHOR

I am so glad you've reached the end of the book and hope you enjoyed it. Thank you for giving me your valuable entertainment time. It is readers like you who make writing such an amazing experience.

If you enjoyed the book, I hope you will leave a review.

Be the First to Know

Want news, pre-order announcements or stuff?

www.SappharíaMayer.com

Want to catch up on all my behind the scenes, current WIPs, side projects and early announcements? Become a Patreon of the Arts.

Sappharia Mayer's Patreons of the Arts

Feel free to reach out to me on any of my social media.

bookbub.com/authors/sappharia-mayer
twitter.com/sapphariamayer
pinterest.com/sapphariamayer
amazon.com/author/sapphariamayer
instagram.com/sapphariamayer

REVEAL ME- CHAPTER 1

EMPYREAN CLUB- THE ATLAS COLLECTION BOOK 2

"Throughout human history, there have been exchanges of power. These exchanges are conceptual and physical, both consensual and non-consensual, but those aren't the terms we use for them on a macro scale. The more recognizable terms are family, clan, community or repression, oppression, oligarchy, dictatorships. Each of these represents an exchange of power. Usually that exchange, in a societal concept, is used for safety, security, or to ensure certain needs are met in our own personal hierarchy. Over time they are encoded into the general societal contract and we forget the nature of the power exchange, translating it to the idea of tradition.

"When we take this exact same concept down to the micro, individual and specific community level, we can see the same situations forming. Two, or more, entities in which basic power is inferred, choosing to exchange it by personal agreement." Professor Dominick Dawes pontificates from the stage in the mid-size lecture hall, which is currently full for his Sexuality Studies graduate seminar.

I find a seat in the crowded room, on the back row, when a male student stands up and motions me over.

The hall smells of a combination of coffee, perfume, and a crowd of bodies. The auditorium style hall's seats curve stadium style, rising from the small stage in the center.

A student's hand shoots up to answer Dominick's question.

"Yes, Angela?" Dominick acknowledges the girl.

"Professor, why would anyone give up power?"

"Good question, Angela. Would you like the answer at a macro or a micro level?"

She sits there for a moment thinking. "A micro one."

"Why are you paying money to be in this class?"

"Because I need a degree and they told me I had to take this one or something like it."

"And why do you need a degree, Angela?"

"To get a better job and make more money."

"And why do you need money?"

"To survive. To pay for food, shelter, clothes."

"And the designer handbags your parents won't buy you if you don't go to class?" He nods to the Gucci bag on the floor.

Her head nods lightly.

"So you have entered into a power exchange agreement with your parents and negotiated the continued supply of the lifestyle to which you've become accustomed for as long as you go to school, maintain the appropriate grade, and ultimately get a degree. Correct?"

"Well, when you put it like that," she huffs.

"And who has the power in this exchange, Angela?"

"My parents do. If they cut me off, I'll be lost."

A smile crosses Dominick's face and he looks out across the room.

"Now we understand how the basic concept of a power exchange is applied in the reality of our worlds. There is no exception in the most primal idea of sex. Often people find it very gratifying to overtly exchange power in a sexual relationship. It is the most personal form of trust and intimacy you can share with other human beings.

"To actually exchange power conceptually, both parties must

come to the table with their own power. So what exactly does that mean?"

The room falls silent as Dominick's eyes search each person. His eyes land on me, his face clouding with a mixture of concern and irritation.

"You, in the very back with the hat. Alexandra, I believe it is." He stares at me for a long minute, as if his eyes are deceiving him. The silence causes the entire class to turn toward me to see what has captivated the attention of their professor.

"Sir, it means that all parties involved must actually know and understand themselves and the nature of the power exchange. In layman's terms, the dominant is driving the car while the submissive navigates. If they do not work in tandem and harmony, then at best, they will get nowhere fast and at worst they will irreparably damage the physical body or relationship. It's not about the abuse of power, which is non-consensual at its very base, but rather about the illusion of control, a place where one readily gives and one readily receives an action. The exchange, as in all exchanges, is in the allowing and participation by both parties."

"Long winded as always, but a very accurate analogy." Dominick nods but his face grows sterner.

The class continues to stare openly at me. The fascinator veil falls dark and low, creating a shadow over half my face. My tailored suit fits my body perfectly, presenting an out of place impeccable image.

The interruption is a curiosity and the obvious personal knowledge between Dominick and me piques the interest of the entire class.

"How does this power exchange change our understanding within the concept of sexuality studies?" He works to bring the class back forward, but I know what is coming next. Dominick could never resist walking the line, playing with his young class' curiosity in sexual studies.

"It depends on the individuals involved," I comment aloud. "It could be that it is a fight for the right to participate in a desired activity. In other places, it could be the interruption of gender roles to provide more fluidity outside of the gender normative world. Then again, we could talk about feminist concepts of equality and gender rights, in what some would identify as a lack of power exchange. Or what about the reverse of 'traditional' power, the most common face of which is the Dominatrix and the submissive male or female," I say, inwardly cringing at the term that aroused stereotypes of women in lingerie and leather, impossibly high heels and wielding a whip, which ultimately has little to do with actually being a professional of the craft.

Frustration crosses Dominick's face. I'm not the same controllable student I was when he took on my mentorship, outside the classroom, while I attended Boston University. It is also quite evident that something is wrong. He hasn't seen me dressed this way since I worked for him on the side, and even then I wouldn't dare go out in public.

"I think that's enough for today. Due next class, find a power exchange and defend it or refute it. Typed. Double spaced. APA styling," he says over the rustle of papers.

I sit quietly, watching the students leave the lecture hall. It hasn't been all that long ago that I'd graced these same hallowed halls daily, in pursuit of a greater life. The turns and directions since were amazing and harrowing at times. Even I have to admit I'm not the same girl that left here. Yet I still feel there's something missing.

The click of the phone's camera is barely audible when I look up, causing everything in me to freeze. This is the exact reason I'd worn this outfit. Just in case the constant click of cameras or video, which everyone seems to want to post for some inane reason, does show up, it won't alert anyone of my location.

Everyone seems to have a camera these days. I hope with half my face in shadow the picture will not reveal who I am when it gets posted. There is no debate on "if" because no matter what, it will always be posted. Unfortunately, I'd not been able to prevent

Dominick from calling my name. At least he'd called the one to match the outfit.

Sitting in his class is a dumb risk. I needed something to give me comfort, and listening to Dominick's lecture always gave me solace. It was something about his baritone voice that made me feel secure.

Dominick was my first dominant and trained me in the mental, physical, and emotional techniques of the trade. He was the father figure who gave me the ability to truly understand the underlying movements of the world, making all of my successes possible. In some ways, it also made my fall inevitable.

For the last several weeks I was off the grid completely. No contact with my staff, my friends, or Reece. It's the only way I could ensure their safety on the heels of being stalked by a client and falling in love with a Dominant, causing an internal war of epic portions.

Nothing in my life felt like my own, but I knew if Kade and Samantha hadn't yet tracked me down, then there was no way for Edmund to do it.

I WATCH THE HALL CLEAR. STUDENTS LINGERING IN CLUSTERS, periodically looking my way and then conversing in low whispers. On the lecture stage, Dominick fields questions from several students, mostly female, who are all vying for his attention. Periodically his eyes lift, looking to make sure I am still waiting. The look in his eyes glues me to my seat. I remember the look. The one he always gave me when I crossed a line or broke a rule. Taking a deep breath, I wonder for the hundredth time if this is the most intelligent decision I've made today.

When the room is cleared, except for a couple of small clusters of students loitering in the back corners of the hall, Dominick motions me to the stage. We stare at each other for a long moment. His eyebrow quirks in a question, and I know I've pushed my luck a bit too far.

Deliberately I stand, smoothing invisible wrinkles in my suit to fortify my resolve. Everything in me is running on empty. Dominick is the one place where I hope I can hide quietly and recharge.

Straightening up to my full height, I step purposefully and gracefully down each row. I look up to the stage when I reach the bottom. Dominick's eyes bore a hole right through me like my sins are open for his full examination. In every possible way, I've been analyzed and evaluated.

"Come," he commands, motioning to the stage with his hand.

My head drops slightly in practiced deference, and I make my way up the short staircase.

He openly looks me up and down, as if he's calculating his next move, taking in all the information currently provided to him.

"Something's wrong," he states.

"Can't I just come visit? I was in the neighborhood..."

"Stop. You can speak again when you can be honest with me," he says, turning on his heel.

I follow. I know what is expected.

We walk in silence across the stage, stepping out of the door from the lecture hall and down the long corridor toward his office.

He unlocks the door and steps inside. The walls of his office are neatly arranged, with boxes marking their contents above the dark mahogany desk set against the wall of large windows. Shelves line two of the walls, full of books from floor to ceiling. I note the marks going down one leg of the desk. They were placed there for each strike I received when I didn't follow directions, broke a rule or generally needed an attitude adjustment. The line of marks runs from the top of the front of the leg to its bottom. My small initials are barely visible under the lip of the desktop.

"Andrea, cancel my office hours. Something's come up unexpectedly and needs my immediate attention," he says into the phone. "I'll need you to cover the lecture on Thursday."

He listens intently to the reply, turning his stern gaze in my direction. It is the same look he gave me right before I made one of the marks going down his desk leg.

"Thank you, Andrea," he says cordially, placing the receiver down.

Cautiously he turns to me, like I'll spook and run away if he moves too fast.

"Does Kade know you're here?"

"No."

His eyebrow raises.

"No, Sir," I amend.

"Does Samantha know you're here?"

"No, Sir."

"Does anyone know you're here?"

I shake my head, letting it fall forward.

"No, Sir."

Dominick runs a hand through his unruly salt and pepper hair in frustration. There is no doubt he is confused at my sudden presence and angry because he doesn't know why. He hates being out of control or outside the circle of knowledge, and in one fell swoop I've created both.

"Did you pilot yourself?" He continues with the interrogation.

"No, Sir."

"Did you take a leave of absence from the PR firm and the club?"

I shake my head, remembering how I'd set my phone on my desk and simply walked away. Guilt washes over me, but it was the only way I knew how to keep everyone safe. I'd already caused Reece's sister's campaign irreparable damage by keeping my secrets. At least this way Edmund couldn't stalk me here, and there'd be no reason for him to attack anyone else I loved.

"I simply walked away without explanation," I admit, blowing out a breath I didn't realize I was holding.

Dominick nods. "I see."

He grabs a couple of stacks of papers and places them in the leather messenger bag I'd given him when I decided to leave for Washington DC. The sight of it leaves me sentimentally torn.

"Come on, girl. Let's get you home. It looks like we've got quite a bit to talk about," he says, walking out of his office. I follow without the need for a command.

We are quiet on the drive from Boston University to Waltham. Each of us is lost in our own thoughts. Periodically he looks over at me, as if he's trying to figure out an enigmatic puzzle. When he parks outside his apartment, it's six in the evening. Lights blaze in the windows, and I feel like I've suddenly interrupted something. He switches off the engine, sitting quietly for a long moment before turning to me.

"Why are you here, Atlas?"

I stare down at my hands, just like I did when I was in school. My fingers knot together, and the emotions I've held down suddenly feel like they will volcanically erupt if I'm not careful.

"I don't know. Right now I just feel scared and lost. After quite a long wander alone in the wilderness, the only place I wanted to go was home," I admit quietly.

Dominick reaches over, taking one of my hands, giving it a gentle squeeze.

"This isn't home, Atlas. Home is in DC, where your entire world can surround you and give you whatever you need. There's something big you're not telling me, girl, but then again, you're not telling anyone. Whatever it is, we'll figure it out together."

I smile softly. Everything in me wants to believe him. Unfortunately, I am long past the moments where I think he's superhuman. Today, the world actually sits completely on my shoulders.

"Before we go inside, I want to remind you the rules didn't change in your absence. Here, you are not my equal. You may stay under my roof, but you know the price," he states simply. "Do you agree to step back into that place?"

"Yes, Sir."

"Do you remember the signals and commands?"

"I believe so," I reply honestly.

"Then my home is open to you. Do you wish to proceed?"

"Yes, Sir. Thank you," I say simply and watch him get out of the car and walk around to my door.

REVEAL ME (THE ATLAS COLLECTION BOOK 3)

Atlas knew her world was crashing around her, so she did the one thing she promised herself she'd never do. She went home. The place where it all started. Where it could cost her the very freedom she craved.

Reece Gabriel is angry. Everything in him feels betrayed. Yet, when his best friend calls and tells him they've located Atlas after she'd been missing for week, he know he had to go find the answers to his questions.

The questions is will he be able to accept what he find when everything about her world is revealed? Or will their connection just be another casualty of her lies?

Pre-order now! Reveal me

ALSO BY SAPPHARIA MAYER

EMPYREAN CLUB SERIES

The Atlas Collection

Mask Me (Book 1)

Master Me (Book 2)

Reveal me (Book 3)

Submit to Me (Book 4)

Play with Me (Book 5)

Mind Games Series - Coming soon!

His Toy Collection

Becoming His Toy

His Toy for the Weekend

His Toy is Going Deeper

His Toy is Trusting Him

ABOUT THE AUTHOR

Sappharia Mayer's erotic romance comes from years of experience in dynamic and various play in the BDSM/Kink lifestyle. She portrays the dance of power exchange relationships with a passion that pushes her characters, and readers, outside their comfort zone, making them squirm, cry, laugh and learn to see things in a whole new way.

Living around the metro area of the nation's capital gives her an up close view of politics and power on a global scale. She loves to delve deep into her worlds and indulge in her various passions, which may or may not include instigating fun *trouble* with her warped sense of humor. If you love romance based in power exchanges with hot kinky sex, then check out Sappharia's books.

www.ingramcontent.com/pod-product-compliance
Lightning Source LLC
Chambersburg PA
CBHW020409210626
46816CB00006BB/2195
9781648930041